**"I don't give up easily.
You should know that."**

Bruno's eyes flamed with anger. "And I'm not going to let you shut me out of my child's life, even if I have to take legal steps to gain access to him."

"You wouldn't dare!"

"Oh, yes I would." Bruno paused to add emphasis. "And I always win any fight I undertake. So you might as well accept the inevitable and marry me."

Norrie smiled coldly. "That's where you're wrong. This is one fight that you don't stand a chance of winning. Because you'll never be able to prove that Ben is yours."

"Is he mine?"

Bruno was making a fool of himself. He seemed so sure, so convinced that Ben was his. Perversely, Norrie decided to play him along a little longer....

Books by Sally Wentworth

These books may be available at your local bookseller.

Don't miss any of our special offers. Write to us at the
following address for information on our newest releases.

Harlequin Reader Service
P.O. Box 52040, Phoenix, AZ 85072-2040
Canadian address: P.O. Box 2800, Postal Station A,
5170 Yonge St., Willowdale, Ont. M2N 6J3

SALLY WENTWORTH

fatal deception

Harlequin Books

TORONTO • NEW YORK • LONDON
AMSTERDAM • PARIS • SYDNEY • HAMBURG
STOCKHOLM • ATHENS • TOKYO • MILAN

Harlequin Presents first edition November 1985
ISBN 0-373-10837-0

Original hardcover edition published in 1985
by Mills & Boon Limited

CHAPTER ONE

THE moment she entered the wide double doorway of the *Welford Observer*, Norrie Peters could tell that something had happened. Neither of the women whose job it was to answer enquiries and take in small ads were at the desk, and the office on the other side of the glass partition sounded different; instead of the clatter of typewriters, there was only the hum of human voices, some of them raised to an angry pitch.

Pushing open the door marked 'STAFF ONLY', Norrie walked into the big office, the level of noise dropping for a moment as everyone looked round, then picking up again as they recognised her and went back to the subject that was so engrossing them.

'What's going on?' she asked one of the reporters standing on the edge of the crowd.

But he only smiled grimly and said, 'You'll find out soon enough,' and turned away to listen to the man next to him.

Mystified and extremely curious, Norrie went out of the main office by the far door and down the corridor to a door marked, 'Sue Stewart, News Editor', knocked and went inside.

Usually at this time on a Monday morning her boss was up to her eyes in work, but today Sue was perched on the edge of her desk, talking to two other full-time employees of the *Observer*. She paused as Norrie came in and said, 'Hi. Have you heard the news?' And before Norrie had time to do more than begin to shake her head, added, 'We're being taken over. They told us this morning. They gave each of us this letter. Here, I've got a copy for you, too.'

Sue passed over an envelope and Norrie quickly read the photocopied letter inside. 'Oh, no,' she groaned. 'This happened to me once before; when I was living down in Devon some years ago.'

'Not by the same people, surely?' one of the other women put in.

'Provincial Press Limited,' Norrie read from the letter's heading. 'No, that was an entirely different company. Have you heard what's going to happen?' she asked quickly, not wanting to bring back memories of that other time, memories that even now could hurt appallingly when they caught her unawares.

'Not really.' Sue shook her head. 'But I suppose that something like this was bound to happen eventually. The paper's been losing money for too long and it either had to go under altogether or else be taken over by a big conglomerate like Provincial Press.'

'Let's just hope they don't make too many changes,' one girl said anxiously; she was saving up to get married and hadn't been there long. 'Mrs Bronwen in Personnel told me that she had to send a list of all the staff over to the head office of Provincial Press at the same time as they looked at the accounts. There's bound to be a shake-up among the staff and the people who came last will be the first to go.'

'Not necessarily,' Sue corrected her. 'They'll probably let the part-timers go first.'

'Thanks,' Norrie said feelingly.

'Oh Lord. Sorry, love.' Sue touched her arm in sympathy. 'And you with young Ben to support. But try not to worry. I'll fight tooth and nail to hang on to you all.'

…s working assiduously today, from the
reception desk, all through the main
… the smaller individual offices of the
…ff in the corridor beyond. Typewriters
… and people moved purposefully about
…rk they were on was of supreme
… far cry from the casual, friendly
…at Norrie usually met. There was a
… of tension in the air and people she'd
… hardly even paused to look up and say
… to her when she greeted them. So the
…obviously arrived and everyone was out
…od impression. Norrie smiled rather
…w she didn't think it would fool him for

…one in her office and looked up
…when Norrie walked in, then relaxed
…elief.

… bag of nerves this morning.' She put
…then automatically reached for another.
…Norrie shook her head. Sue said, 'Oh,
…u don't, do you? I must have smoked
…eady and it's only half past nine.'

… new management's representative has
… said sympathetically.

…s,' Sue answered feelingly. 'He was in
… us at eight o'clock yesterday morning.
… nearly died when he came in at eight-
…d that the wretched man was there
…arry thought he'd be here first, of
…ld put on an act of being dedicated to

…was,' Norrie observed mildly.
…eply on her cigarette. 'Only when it
…likes the perks that go with the job:

'It wouldn't make any difference,' Norrie told her with remembered bitterness. 'People from big companies like Provincial Press don't have any feelings, they don't care who they hurt so long as they make a profit. Their only god is money.'

Her feelings came through so strongly that the other three women looked at her silently for a moment, taken aback by the venom in her voice, but then Sue recovered and asked, 'Does anyone know who they're sending down?'

'No, but Mrs Bronwen said that someone would be arriving tomorrow.'

'Well, take-over or not, the paper still has to be got out on Friday, so we'd better get to work.'

But there was too much apprehension and anticipation running through the old Victorian building that housed the newspaper office for much work to be done that day. Everyone wanted to talk it over with everyone else, and it was only when Harry Simons, the editor, came and told them all to get on with it, that even a semblance of normal order returned to the place.

As a part-time features writer, Norrie could go into the office more or less when she liked, but when she had first started working for the *Observer* two years ago, she had got into the routine of going in on Monday and Wednesday mornings; Mondays to hand in her copy and Wednesdays to discuss new feature ideas. The rest of the week she worked on her own initiative, researching the features and writing them up, in between looking after Ben. At first she had had to pay someone to take care of him while she'd gone to the office, but for the past year he had gone to nursery school three mornings a week, which had helped a great deal. At twelve Norrie went along to collect him, still thinking about the take-over and worried that she might lose the regular work the *Observer* gave her. She wrote for other outlets where she could, magazine articles and short stories mostly, but very little of that was commissioned and it was a bonus if it got accepted. Of course she wasn't exactly penniless; Geoff sent her money regularly every month and there was some money that her father had left her, but most of that had gone on buying the cottage and she didn't want to have to break into the balance if she could possibly avoid it. And not only that, she needed to work to keep her mind active and alert; she'd go mad if she had nothing to do all day except chat to a toddler whose conversation, although surprising at times, wasn't exactly stimulating.

Norrie reached the nursery school, which was only a quarter of a mile or so from the High Street, and joined the crowd of mums waiting inside the gates for their offspring. They all thought that Ben was hers and Norrie didn't bother to enlighten them; she had taken Ben over on the day he was born, the day his own mother had died and his father, her elder brother Geoff, had rejected him, and now all they had was each other.

She grinned at him as the children came bursting out of the building and he ran across the grass towards her. He was nearly four now and considered himself too big to be helped, but his fat little fingers couldn't manage the zip of his anorak so that it blew out around him as he ran. 'Hi. Had a good morning?' She zipped him up while he proudly showed her his drawing of a van being chased by a police car. He certainly didn't have any hang-ups; he was a normal bloodthirsty little boy. Norrie took his hand and they walked home to the cottage, Ben chattering away asking dozens of

questions, a habit
regretted as she str
met with another q
When they got h
sat down to read th
had his sleep, but
the take-over and t
to that other take-o
ago now, when her
local paper and sh
reporter in her ver
losing too much mo
behind everyone's b
Holdings, and they
Norrie threw the
hands to her face. S
back to that time.
forget him, that was
pain had worn off ar
of her mind, never
brought it all floodin
that was silly, she sc
be afraid of this time
entirely different c
personnel. No one th
life and leave it emp
On Wednesday, N
mixed feelings, wor
although reason told
the new management
people moved fast th
list and the accounts
could have made up
to get rid of even be
foot through the door

Everyone w
women on th
office and in
more senior s
clacked busil
as if the w
importance;
atmosphere
definite feelin
known for ye
good mornin
new man had
to make a
wryly; some
a minute.
Sue was
apprehensive
with a sigh o
'God, I'm
out a cigaret
'Want a fag
that's right,
half a dozen
'I gather
arrived?' No
'I'll say h
here waiting
Poor old H
thirty and
before him
course, and
the paper.'
'I though
Sue drev
suits him.

being invited to join the Rotary Club, giving talks and that kind of thing. Being a big fish in a small pond, I suppose. But he spends too much time on that and not enough on improving the circulation figures.'

Norrie looked at the other woman in some surprise; she'd never heard her criticise anyone at the office before. Sue was nearly forty, about fifteen years older than herself, divorced, and with several boyfriends in her past—and present probably—and had come to the *Observer* straight from a London paper when she had moved into the area because of her husband's job many years ago. There were rumours that her husband making her leave London had caused the break-up of their marriage, but the two women didn't know each other well enough to confide in each other, and whether Sue stayed in Welford because she wanted to or because she couldn't get back into Fleet Street, no one really knew.

'Has anyone heard anything yet?' Norrie asked to change the subject, not wanting to talk about Harry behind his back.

Sue shook her head. 'Nothing definite. All the editors have been asked to submit reports on the people under them together with samples of their work if applicable. So I suppose Harry has been asked to do the same with the sub-editors,' she said grimly. 'But all day yesterday he was busy showing the man from Provincial Press round the place, introducing him to everyone and explaining how everything works. Not that he looked as if he needed to be told anything,' she added with a grimace.

'Why, what's he like?'

Stubbing out her cigarette viciously, Sue gave a short, unmirthful laugh. 'An arrogant bastard. Cold as hell. But quite youngish and damn good-looking

though. In other circumstances . . .' She shrugged.
'But he's so formal and distant you wouldn't believe.
That icy kind of politeness that makes you feel as if
you've crawled up out of a hole, you know?'

'He sounds ghastly,' Norrie agreed with a shudder.
'What's his name?'

'Er—Fenton, I think. No, Denton, that was it.
Bruno Denton.' Sue looked up when Norrie didn't
speak and her mouth opened in astonishment. 'Why
Norrie, what on earth's the matter? Are you ill? You're
as white as a sheet.'

There was a spare chair by the desk and Norrie
collapsed into it, the room gyrating around her. She
was aware that Sue was talking to her but couldn't
hear properly for the roaring in her ears. Waves of
blackness came up to meet her and she would have
passed out except that Sue pushed her head down
between her knees and then thrust a bottle of smelling
salts under her nose, making her eyes water as she
tried to flinch away.

'Is that better? Are you okay? Or do you want me to
send for a doctor?' Sue asked anxiously, the open
bottle of smelling-salts hovering near Norrie's face.

'No. No, I'm all right.' She pushed Sue's hand
away.

'What on earth happened? Did you suddenly feel
faint?'

'It was . . .' For a moment Norrie almost blurted out
the truth, but thankfully came to her senses enough to
realise how stupid that would be. Instead she nodded
and stammered, 'Everything seemed to go round
suddenly.'

Sue put a hand on her forehead, looking at her
worriedly. 'Well, you don't feel hot or anything. Are
you getting enough to eat?' she demanded.

'What? Oh yes, of course. Perhaps I've got a cold coming or something.' Norrie straightened up. 'Sorry. That was stupid.'

'Don't be silly. You'd better go home and go to bed. You haven't got a car, have you? I'll get someone to drive you home.'

'Oh no, please, that isn't necessary. I feel fine now. Honestly,' Norrie assured her.

'Well, you don't look fine. You look as if you've seen a ghost.'

No, not seen one, Norrie thought bitterly, just heard that one I hoped was laid had been resurrected.

'I suppose you've been worrying yourself sick in case you lose your work here,' Sue said admonishingly.

'I expect we all have,' Norrie answered, getting to her feet. She was more in control of herself now but wanted desperately to get away, to get out of this building and put as much space between it and herself as possible.

'Yes, but some of us have more responsibilities than others,' Sue remarked, referring to Ben. She crossed to pick up the internal 'phone. 'I'll ask one of the reporters to take you home.'

'No, please. I'd much rather go alone.'

'All right,' Sue agreed but with a puzzled frown. 'Look, if you're short I can let you have some money to . . .'

Norrie flushed, bright spots of colour filling her pale cheeks. 'It isn't that, *really*. I'm loaded.'

'Well, if you're sure,' Sue agreed reluctantly. 'But promise me you'll go to the café across the road and have something to eat before you go home?'

'Yes, okay.' Norrie somehow managed the travesty of a smile and edged towards the door. 'If you say so.'

'I insist. And don't worry about submitting any work this week. I've got enough features in hand to cover.'

'Okay, thanks.'

At last Norrie was out of the office. She ran down the corridor but saw the door of the Editor's office opening and the sound of voices, so she turned on her heel and dived into the ladies' cloakroom, her heart palpitating with fear. Luckily there was no one else in there and she was able to lean against the wall until her heart stopped racing quite so much. Oh God, she thought miserably, why did it have to be him? *Why, why, why?* Of all the places in the world why did he have to come here? When I was so settled and starting to make a life for myself again. Bruno Denton. His name rang in her ears. But how? Before, he had been working for a different company. He must have changed his job or something. Norrie's stunned brain tried to grapple with the situation but she was too distraught to think straight. She would have to leave the *Observer*, that was certain; she couldn't possibly risk coming into the office again while he was here. But perhaps she could get her assignments by 'phone and send the copy through the post, then he'd never know that she was working there. But then Norrie remembered the staff list he'd been given and the reports that Bruno had asked for and her heart sank again. He must already know that she worked for the *Observer*. The room began to sway again until suddenly cold cynicism took over. If he even remembered her name. If she wasn't just one in a long line of women that he'd used to further his ambitions—and to satisfy his bodily needs into the bargain, she thought with world-weary bitterness.

Slowly Norrie straightened up and looked at herself

'It wouldn't make any difference,' Norrie told her with remembered bitterness. 'People from big companies like Provincial Press don't have any feelings, they don't care who they hurt so long as they make a profit. Their only god is money.'

Her feelings came through so strongly that the other three women looked at her silently for a moment, taken aback by the venom in her voice, but then Sue recovered and asked, 'Does anyone know who they're sending down?'

'No, but Mrs Bronwen said that someone would be arriving tomorrow.'

'Well, take-over or not, the paper still has to be got out on Friday, so we'd better get to work.'

But there was too much apprehension and anticipation running through the old Victorian building that housed the newspaper office for much work to be done that day. Everyone wanted to talk it over with everyone else, and it was only when Harry Simons, the editor, came and told them all to get on with it, that even a semblance of normal order returned to the place.

As a part-time features writer, Norrie could go into the office more or less when she liked, but when she had first started working for the *Observer* two years ago, she had got into the routine of going in on Monday and Wednesday mornings; Mondays to hand in her copy and Wednesdays to discuss new feature ideas. The rest of the week she worked on her own initiative, researching the features and writing them up, in between looking after Ben. At first she had had to pay someone to take care of him while she'd gone to the office, but for the past year he had gone to nursery school three mornings a week, which had helped a great deal. At twelve Norrie went along to collect him, still thinking about the take-over and worried that she might lose the regular work the *Observer* gave her. She wrote for other outlets where she could, magazine articles and short stories mostly, but very little of that was commissioned and it was a bonus if it got accepted. Of course she wasn't exactly penniless; Geoff sent her money regularly every month and there was some money that her father had left her, but most of that had gone on buying the cottage and she didn't want to have to break into the balance if she could possibly avoid it. And not only that, she needed to work to keep her mind active and alert; she'd go mad if she had nothing to do all day except chat to a toddler whose conversation, although surprising at times, wasn't exactly stimulating.

Norrie reached the nursery school, which was only a quarter of a mile or so from the High Street, and joined the crowd of mums waiting inside the gates for their offspring. They all thought that Ben was hers and Norrie didn't bother to enlighten them; she had taken Ben over on the day he was born, the day his own mother had died and his father, her elder brother Geoff, had rejected him, and now all they had was each other.

She grinned at him as the children came bursting out of the building and he ran across the grass towards her. He was nearly four now and considered himself too big to be helped, but his fat little fingers couldn't manage the zip of his anorak so that it blew out around him as he ran. 'Hi. Had a good morning?' She zipped him up while he proudly showed her his drawing of a van being chased by a police car. He certainly didn't have any hang-ups; he was a normal bloodthirsty little boy. Norrie took his hand and they walked home to the cottage, Ben chattering away asking dozens of questions, a habit she encouraged in him but often regretted as she struggled to find an answer, only to be met with another question two seconds later.

When they got home, Norrie made lunch and then sat down to read the paper for ten minutes while Ben had his sleep, but her thoughts kept coming back to the take-over and then, inevitably, even further back to that other take-over back in Devon, over four years ago now, when her father had been the editor of the local paper and she was working on it as a junior reporter in her very first job. The paper had been losing too much money and the owners had sold out behind everyone's backs to a company called Westland Holdings, and they had sent . . .

Norrie threw the paper aside abruptly and put her hands to her face. She wouldn't!' She wouldn't think back to that time. To that man. She would never forget him, that was impossible, but at least the raw pain had worn off and she'd been able to put him out of her mind, nevertheless this morning's news had brought it all flooding back, the pain and the fear. But that was silly, she scolded herself; there was nothing to be afraid of this time—except losing her job—it was an entirely different company with entirely different personnel. No one this time would come to disrupt her life and leave it empty and in ashes.

On Wednesday, Norrie went to the office with very mixed feelings, wondering if she still had a job, although reason told her that it was too soon yet for the new management to have made any decisions. But people moved fast these days and they'd had the staff list and the accounts for some weeks, the management could have made up their minds who they were going to get rid of even before their representative had set foot through the door.

Everyone was working assiduously today, from the women on the reception desk, all through the main office and into the smaller individual offices of the more senior staff in the corridor beyond. Typewriters clacked busily and people moved purposefully about as if the work they were on was of supreme importance; a far cry from the casual, friendly atmosphere that Norrie usually met. There was a definite feeling of tension in the air and people she'd known for years hardly even paused to look up and say good morning to her when she greeted them. So the new man had obviously arrived and everyone was out to make a good impression. Norrie smiled rather wryly; somehow she didn't think it would fool him for a minute.

Sue was alone in her office and looked up apprehensively when Norrie walked in, then relaxed with a sigh of relief.

'God, I'm a bag of nerves this morning.' She put out a cigarette, then automatically reached for another. 'Want a fag?' Norrie shook her head. Sue said, 'Oh, that's right, you don't, do you? I must have smoked half a dozen already and it's only half past nine.'

'I gather the new management's representative has arrived?' Norrie said sympathetically.

'I'll say he has,' Sue answered feelingly. 'He was in here waiting for us at eight o'clock yesterday morning. Poor old Harry nearly died when he came in at eight-thirty and found that the wretched man was there before him; Harry thought he'd be here first, of course, and could put on an act of being dedicated to the paper.'

'I thought he was,' Norrie observed mildly.

Sue drew deeply on her cigarette. 'Only when it suits him. He likes the perks that go with the job:

being invited to join the Rotary Club, giving talks and that kind of thing. Being a big fish in a small pond, I suppose. But he spends too much time on that and not enough on improving the circulation figures.'

Norrie looked at the other woman in some surprise; she'd never heard her criticise anyone at the office before. Sue was nearly forty, about fifteen years older than herself, divorced, and with several boyfriends in her past—and present probably—and had come to the *Observer* straight from a London paper when she had moved into the area because of her husband's job many years ago. There were rumours that her husband making her leave London had caused the break-up of their marriage, but the two women didn't know each other well enough to confide in each other, and whether Sue stayed in Welford because she wanted to or because she couldn't get back into Fleet Street, no one really knew.

'Has anyone heard anything yet?' Norrie asked to change the subject, not wanting to talk about Harry behind his back.

Sue shook her head. 'Nothing definite. All the editors have been asked to submit reports on the people under them together with samples of their work if applicable. So I suppose Harry has been asked to do the same with the sub-editors,' she said grimly. 'But all day yesterday he was busy showing the man from Provincial Press round the place, introducing him to everyone and explaining how everything works. Not that he looked as if he needed to be told anything,' she added with a grimace.

'Why, what's he like?'

Stubbing out her cigarette viciously, Sue gave a short, unmirthful laugh. 'An arrogant bastard. Cold as hell. But quite youngish and damn good-looking

though. In other circumstances . . .' She shrugged.
'But he's so formal and distant you wouldn't believe.
That icy kind of politeness that makes you feel as if
you've crawled up out of a hole, you know?'

'He sounds ghastly,' Norrie agreed with a shudder.
'What's his name?'

'Er—Fenton, I think. No, Denton, that was it.
Bruno Denton.' Sue looked up when Norrie didn't
speak and her mouth opened in astonishment. 'Why
Norrie, what on earth's the matter? Are you ill? You're
as white as a sheet.'

There was a spare chair by the desk and Norrie
collapsed into it, the room gyrating around her. She
was aware that Sue was talking to her but couldn't
hear properly for the roaring in her ears. Waves of
blackness came up to meet her and she would have
passed out except that Sue pushed her head down
between her knees and then thrust a bottle of smelling
salts under her nose, making her eyes water as she
tried to flinch away.

'Is that better? Are you okay? Or do you want me to
send for a doctor?' Sue asked anxiously, the open
bottle of smelling-salts hovering near Norrie's face.

'No. No, I'm all right.' She pushed Sue's hand
away.

'What on earth happened? Did you suddenly feel
faint?'

'It was . . .' For a moment Norrie almost blurted out
the truth, but thankfully came to her senses enough to
realise how stupid that would be. Instead she nodded
and stammered, 'Everything seemed to go round
suddenly.'

Sue put a hand on her forehead, looking at her
worriedly. 'Well, you don't feel hot or anything. Are
you getting enough to eat?' she demanded.

'What? Oh yes, of course. Perhaps I've got a cold coming or something.' Norrie straightened up. 'Sorry. That was stupid.'

'Don't be silly. You'd better go home and go to bed. You haven't got a car, have you? I'll get someone to drive you home.'

'Oh no, please, that isn't necessary. I feel fine now. Honestly,' Norrie assured her.

'Well, you don't look fine. You look as if you've seen a ghost.'

No, not seen one, Norrie thought bitterly, just heard that one I hoped was laid had been resurrected.

'I suppose you've been worrying yourself sick in case you lose your work here,' Sue said admonishingly.

'I expect we all have,' Norrie answered, getting to her feet. She was more in control of herself now but wanted desperately to get away, to get out of this building and put as much space between it and herself as possible.

'Yes, but some of us have more responsibilities than others,' Sue remarked, referring to Ben. She crossed to pick up the internal 'phone. 'I'll ask one of the reporters to take you home.'

'No, *please*. I'd much rather go alone.'

'All right,' Sue agreed but with a puzzled frown. 'Look, if you're short I can let you have some money to . . .'

Norrie flushed, bright spots of colour filling her pale cheeks. 'It isn't that, *really*. I'm loaded.'

'Well, if you're sure,' Sue agreed reluctantly. 'But promise me you'll go to the café across the road and have something to eat before you go home?'

'Yes, okay.' Norrie somehow managed the travesty of a smile and edged towards the door. 'If you say so.'

'I insist. And don't worry about submitting any
work this week. I've got enough features in hand to
cover.'

'Okay, thanks.'

At last Norrie was out of the office. She ran down
the corridor but saw the door of the Editor's office
opening and the sound of voices, so she turned on her
heel and dived into the ladies' cloakroom, her heart
palpitating with fear. Luckily there was no one else in
there and she was able to lean against the wall until
her heart stopped racing quite so much. Oh God, she
thought miserably, why did it have to be him? *Why,
why, why?* Of all the places in the world why did he
have to come here? When I was so settled and starting
to make a life for myself again. Bruno Denton. His
name rang in her ears. But how? Before, he had been
working for a different company. He must have
changed his job or something. Norrie's stunned brain
tried to grapple with the situation but she was too
distraught to think straight. She would have to leave
the *Observer*, that was certain; she couldn't possibly
risk coming into the office again while he was here.
But perhaps she could get her assignments by 'phone
and send the copy through the post, then he'd never
know that she was working there. But then Norrie
remembered the staff list he'd been given and the
reports that Bruno had asked for and her heart sank
again. He must already know that she worked for the
Observer. The room began to sway again until
suddenly cold cynicism took over. If he even
remembered her name. If she wasn't just one in a long
line of women that he'd used to further his
ambitions—and to satisfy his bodily needs into the
bargain, she thought with world-weary bitterness.

Slowly Norrie straightened up and looked at herself

in the mirror; her mascara had run and she didn't have any with her to repair it. So she washed her face and ran a comb through her soft fair hair, unaware that her paleness emphasised the beauty of her long-lashed grey eyes. She had to leave the sanctuary of the cloakroom sometime. Reluctantly Norrie opened the door a little and listened, but the corridor was quiet with only the sound of distant voices coming from one of the offices down the far end. Summoning up all her courage, she stepped out and hurried into the main office, walking through it with her head down, praying that Bruno wouldn't be in there and see her. She reached the far door safely and gave a shuddering sigh of relief as she went through into the reception area.

The kind of luck she'd been having the last few years, she ought to have known that nothing could go right. As she stepped towards the main door and safety, two men came in. Harry Simons, the editor, and beside him Bruno Denton. He saw her immediately and paused. So at least he remembered her. She tried to look past him, but her eyes were drawn to his face as to a magnet and met his for a searing moment that seemed to last for eternity. Somehow she managed to turn her head away and move to walk past him, but he put out an arm to stop her.

She stopped a couple of inches away from his arm, making sure it didn't touch her, and kept her head averted.

'Norrie?'

Slowly she turned to look at him, her gaze meant to freeze him. He hadn't changed much in the four and a half years since she'd told him to get the hell out of her life. Not physically anyway. There were a couple of lines around his mouth that hadn't been there before, but that was all. God, could she really remember his face that well after all this time? But when you'd been so much in love with a man that you'd delighted in kissing every pore of his skin . . .

'It's good to see you again,' Bruno was saying slowly. 'It's been a long time.'

Norrie's chin came up. 'But not long enough.'

His face hardened and he dropped his arm. 'I see you haven't changed.'

'And nor have you,' she countered coldly. 'Your being here proves that. You're still in the destruction business.'

'I'm merely doing my job.'

'Oh, sure. That's what the Gestapo said when they sent people to the gas chambers.' She stepped forward to go by him, but now Harry Simons was in her way.

'You two seem to know each other,' he observed, making no effort to conceal his surprise and annoyance as he looked at Norrie.

'Why yes, we know each other from—way back,' Bruno answered. Adding, 'But please don't be swayed by Miss Peters's opinions. Although harmless, she is inclined to base her assumptions on hearsay rather than truth.' Then, before Norrie could think of a suitable retort, he walked on into the office with Harry following at his heels like a dog.

Furious at his parting shot, Norrie stepped out on to the pavement and turned to walk blindly along the High Street, again railing against the fate that had brought Bruno to Welford. It had been so long ago and so far away; she'd really thought that she was rid of him for ever. But now he had turned up again to break her fragile hold on happiness at the very least. And at the most—Norrie shuddered as she remembered how

Bruno had ruined her life before.

The pungent smell of manure drifted across on the breeze and Norrie realised that she had walked all the way to the cattle market. It was held every Wednesday, the stalls in the big sheds standing empty the rest of the week. Some pigs were being herded into a farm truck ready to be driven away, large purple numbers painted on their pink backs. The driver hailed her as she wandered over; she'd done a feature about the market only a couple of months ago and had got to know most of the men working there.

She stood for a while amid the noise and bustle as the auctioneers conducted the sale, seeming to take bids out of the air as they moved slowly down the rows of penned animals. There was a small hut used as a snack bar attached to the market and Norrie went inside and bought herself a cup of tea. The cup was chipped but the tea was good and strong and she swallowed it thirstily, wishing it was something a lot stronger. She was glad she was angry, Norrie decided. Glad that, if she'd had to meet Bruno at all, she'd met him head on, the old hatred and bitterness welling up to make her hit out at him. Although she very much doubted that she'd hurt him at all. She gave a mental laugh of self-derision; if anyone got hurt it would be herself. After this morning's little episode, if Bruno hadn't already decided to sack her then Harry undoubtedly would. He'd looked mad as fire when she'd been so openly rude to Bruno, whom he was obviously trying to keep sweet.

Leaning back against the wooden wall of the snack bar, Norrie closed her eyes and tried to think what to do as emotionlessly as possible. Not that it had ever been possible where Bruno was concerned. She had fallen disastrously in love with him the moment she'd met him when she was only nineteen, gladly giving him whatever he'd wanted: her body, her soul, and the information he'd needed to ruin her father. A year later her father had died in a car crash that involved no one else and was officially an accident, but which Norrie was quite certain had been suicide. She wondered if Bruno knew that her father was dead, whether he cared.

Her first instinct on hearing his name was to run, as far away as possible. But she had done that once and he had come back into her life; the world of local newspapers was the only one she knew and wasn't that large, even if she went away it was possible she might meet him again eventually. Although it wasn't a possibility that she'd envisaged before now, otherwise she might never have come to work for the *Observer*. And anyway, why run? She wasn't the one who had anything to feel guilty about. Better, surely, to stay and face him, to get him out of her system once and for all?

That was the logical and sensible way to behave of course, but Norrie wasn't sure that she had the courage to do it, she would much rather be a coward and run. She *must* be able to get some other kind of work, in an office or a shop or something. But her soul cringed away from being stuck inside all day long; she was used to getting out and about and would find the loss of her freedom very hard to bear. Then there was the problem of Ben. If she took any other kind of job she would have to pay for him to be looked after all day, and although her brother gave her quite enough to pay for Ben's keep, she knew that Geoff was saving up to start his own business when he came back to England and she was reluctant to ask him for more money.

'Oh, damn Bruno Denton! Damn him, damn him, damn him!' she exclaimed aloud, making the two farmers who were in the snack bar turn and grin as they looked at her.

One said jocularly, 'Tell us who he is, lass, and we'll set the bull on him.'

'I wish you could,' Norrie said feelingly, liking the idea a great deal.

Moodily she put down her cup and walked back through the town again, still angry as she thought of all the changes Bruno had made to her life and the people she had worked with back in Devon. And they had just stood back and let it happen, as the people on the *Observer* probably would unless someone got them together to stand up to Bruno and his so-called reforms. Not that she could see anyone taking on the task; Welford was a comfortably sleepy town and the staff on the *Observer* weren't exactly the militant types, even though they all belonged to the print union. They were all probably hoping against hope that they would keep their jobs, and wouldn't want to start anything in case they were looked on as troublemakers and were the first to go. Or perhaps they didn't think they were in any danger. But then they didn't know the way Bruno worked and how ruthless he could be to get what he wanted. Only Norrie knew that. So maybe it was up to her to tell her colleagues, to stir them into putting up some sort of resistance so that Bruno didn't just tread them into oblivion as he had the staff in Devon.

Norrie stood still and gazed at her reflection in a shop window. She saw a tall, slim girl of twenty-four years old, with curly fair hair and not a bad face, attractive enough to draw a few wolf whistles anyway. But did she have what it took to rouse the people at the *Observer* to fight Bruno? She was certainly angry enough; all the old hate and bitterness had come seething back just at the sound of his name, like a volcano that had lain dormant for years and had suddenly erupted again with increased violence. If she told them what had happened in Devon and passed that anger on ... And it would certainly give her a great deal of satisfaction to put a spoke in Bruno's wheel, to stop him from getting an easy victory. She smiled to herself and for a moment she was startled; that reflected smile had looked really nasty. But then Norrie shrugged and tossed her head as she turned away. So what the hell? Bruno deserved everything he got, and much, much more. Nothing she could do to him would ever make up for the evil he had done to her and her father.

Glancing at her watch, Norrie saw that it was nearly eleven, which gave almost a whole hour before she went to collect Ben. You could do a lot in an hour. Determined now on what she was going to do, she started to walk briskly back towards the *Observer* offices.

In the printing industry the union representatives are usually known as 'The Father of the Chapel', a Chapel being a printing firm. At the *Observer* the Father of the Chapel was called Ted Burtenshaw; he was a man of about fifty-five who had been in printing all his life and who did little more than preside over the quarterly meetings, collect the dues when you joined, and get drunk at the annual binge. Norrie sought him out in the linotype room. 'Got a few minutes to spare, Ted?'

As all he was doing was standing and having a cigarette, he nodded and came over. 'What's up?'

'I'd like to have a quiet word with you, about this

company that's taking us over. And about Bruno Denton.'

Ted's eyes lit with curiosity. 'You know something?' he asked, walking to a quiet corner of the big room, away from the other men.

Norrie nodded. 'Quite a bit—and none of it good. You see, I used to work on a paper in Devon . . .' She talked rapidly, stressing Bruno's roughshod methods but being very careful not to mention her own emotional involvement with him.

Ted's eyes widened in amazement and his usually placid face grew red. 'Are you sure of all this?'

'Of course I'm sure. I was there. You can check the facts for yourself if you want. It happened over four and a half years ago, and the name of the paper was the *Westland Gazette*.'

'But you say Denton was working for a different company then?'

'Yes, he was,' Norrie admitted. 'But the man's the same, Ted. He hasn't changed.'

'No, I see what you mean.' Ted stroked his chin. 'Thanks for telling me. We'll have to do something about this.'

'What will you do?' Norrie urged. 'Call a meeting? I'd like to come to it.'

'Yes, you must. The others will want to know. Yes, I suppose we'd better have an emergency meeting. I was going to wait until after we'd heard a bit more, but now . . . Well, this puts a different complexion on things. I'll have a word with some of the lads first though. And I'd better find out what I can about this firm that's taking us over. We don't want to go off half cock,' he said with all his native caution.

Norrie looked at him rather frustratedly, knowing that she wasn't going to get any further with him for

the time being. But there was more than one way to
kill a cat . . . She left him and walked back through to
the offices.

'Hey, I thought I told you to go home,' Sue
exclaimed when Norrie put her head into her office.

'I changed my mind. Are you doing anything for
lunch?'

'Nothing that can't be shelved.' Sue looked at her
speculatively. 'I hear you had a brush with the new
broom this morning. Couldn't be something to do
with that, could it?'

After wincing at the pun, Norrie nodded and said,
'It could be at that. Interested?'

'I'll say. Where and when?'

'I've got to go and collect Ben now, but I'll meet
you at the Welford Arms at twelve-thirty.'

'The Lord Nelson's nearer,' Sue objected.

'Yes, but it doesn't have a garden. I can't take Ben
into the pub so we'll have to eat outside. Okay?'

'Okay, but it had better be good.'

'The food or the story?'

'The story of course.'

Norrie laughed. 'I know you'll be interested, but I
don't think you're going to like it. See you, I've got to
run or I'll be late for Ben.'

And Norrie literally had to run, arriving at the
nursery school just as Ben was beginning to look
uncertainly round for her, his cheeky face breaking
into a big grin when she came in the gate.

'We were beginning to think you weren't going to
make it,' the nursery teacher scolded.

'Sorry. Got delayed,' Norrie panted.

'We can take Ben five mornings a week when the
new term starts,' the woman offered. 'Someone's
moving away so there'll be a place.'

'That's great. You'd like that wouldn't you Ben?' There was just a trace of anxiety in Norrie's tone.

'Will Debbie and Sara be here?' Ben demanded.

Norrie grinned. 'Of course.'

'He's after the girls already,' the teacher laughed.

'Just like his father,' Norrie remarked unthinkingly, then caught a quick glance from the teacher that made her giggle as she walked away. Now it would probably be all over the town that Ben's father was a sex-maniac. Which was far from the truth, she thought, sobering suddenly. Geoff had enjoyed going out with girls, certainly, and had had a great variety of them until he had met Janet and fallen deeply in love with her. But Janet had died after only a few years of marriage and as far as Norrie knew Geoff hadn't looked at another woman since, going to Saudi Arabia to bury himself in his work. And leaving Norrie to hold the baby! But who cared when he was as adorable as Ben. She bent suddenly and gave the child a big hug. He suffered it, smugly aware—as all children are—that he was totally irresistible.

'Come on,' she told him, straightening up and taking his hand. 'We're having a treat today. We're going to have lunch at the pub.'

His eyes grew round at that and he strutted importantly along beside her, taking as big a step as he could manage.

They found a good table, in the sun but sheltered from the breeze by a wall. 'Can I have beer?' Ben demanded.

'No, but you may have Coke, which is fizzy like beer. A sort of children's beer. But we have to wait for a friend to arrive first.'

Sue turned up about ten minutes later and looked after Ben while Norrie went inside to buy the drinks and order the food. When she came out the two of them were deep in conversation about space rockets, which were Ben's favourite thing at the moment, and Norrie couldn't get a word in until Ben was tucking into his scampi and chips.

'Wow!' Sue exclaimed. 'Doesn't he ever stop talking?'

'Not often,' Norrie admitted. 'But I don't like to shut him up too much.'

'He'd probably burst with frustration if you did. He's very intelligent, though.' She looked wistful for a moment. 'You're lucky to have him.' Sue hadn't any children of her own.

Norrie smiled at her warmly. 'Yes, I know.'

'Even in the circumstances?' Sue asked, raising an eyebrow.

'What circumstances?'

'Not being married.'

'In any circumstances,' Norrie said firmly. It was the first time that Sue had ever asked even the most casual question about Ben, and Norrie didn't see why she should enlighten her. Anyway, she liked to think of Ben as her own; he was all she had. 'Now, about Bruno Denton,' she began.

'Of course.' Sue sat forward eagerly. 'Give. It was all over the office about your clash with him this morning. The girls on the desk saw all and, as you can well imagine, they were telling everyone else within minutes. It seems you know him quite well?'

'Well enough to hate him,' Norrie told her feelingly.

'Really? Is that why you nearly passed out this morning? When you heard that he was here?' Sue asked shrewdly.

'Hearing his name did come as rather a shock, I

admit. You didn't tell anyone, did you?' she added anxiously.

Sue shook her head. 'No, I didn't connect the two until you came back to the office. How did you meet him?'

'The company he was working for at the time took over the paper I was working on in Devon some years ago. They sent him along to put it back on its feet. He did, but in the process he also put several people out of work, most of whom had worked on the paper for years. Okay, maybe some of them were past it. But it was the way he did it, so cruelly, without any regard for their feelings. One of them even committed suicide a year later.'

'No! Who was he?'

'He was the editor. And as it happens he was also my father.'

'Norrie! You mean to say that . . .? Good God, I said he was a cold bastard, but I didn't think that . . .' Sue stopped, at a temporary loss for words until she said, 'No wonder you hate him!'

'Quite. But the point is, will he do the same to the *Observer* as he did to my father's paper?'

'Lord, yes. Tell me exactly what happened.'

So Norrie went through it again, ending, 'I've already talked to Ted Burtenshaw and told him all this, but you know how slow he is; I thought I'd better tell someone in the office as well, so as you're my boss . . .'

'And you were right. Your Bruno Denton needn't think he can ride roughshod over . . .'

'He isn't *my* Bruno Denton,' Norrie interrupted sharply.

Sue looked at her in surprise and again that speculative look came into her eyes. 'How long ago did you say all this happened?'

'More than four years ago.'

'Yes.' Sue's gaze fell fleetingly on Ben. 'Of course Denton's a very good-looking devil. I expect he more or less charmed his way in before he showed his ruthless side?'

'Something like that,' Norrie admitted slowly, turning her head away.

To her relief Sue didn't pursue the subject, instead discussing ways and means of handling the situation. Norrie was glad to let her take over, knowing that Sue was far more experienced than she was, and encouraging her to be as militant as possible. After a while, though, Ben started to get restless and fretful; he was tired and wanted to have his sleep, so the two women parted with Sue promising to ginger up Ted and do what she could among the rest of the staff. Norrie carried Ben home and by the time they got there he was asleep on her shoulder; she laid him down on his bed and rubbed her arm; he was getting too heavy to carry any great distance. He looked so innocent when he was asleep, a far cry from the imp of mischief he was when awake. He had her brother's fair hair and grey eyes, as were Norrie's, and she often saw Geoff in him, but there was nothing of his mother, not that Norrie could really remember Janet very well after all these years, although she conscientiously kept a photograph of her on display for Ben's sake, but so far he had shown little curiosity about it and Norrie didn't push it.

Later that afternoon, Sue rang and said that Ted Burtenshaw had arranged an emergency union meeting for ten the next morning and they wanted Norrie to be there, which she promised she would. It meant having to pay someone to look after Ben, but it was a small price to pay to annoy Bruno, although she hoped that the outcome of the meeting would do a whole lot more than just annoy him.

That evening Norrie went through the suitcase containing all her father's papers, sorting out all the written evidence she could find to back up her story about the *Westland Gazette*: written statements from sacked members of the staff, copies of union meeting minutes, that kind of thing. She wanted to make her case as strong as she possibly could, knowing that she might eventually have to face Bruno with it. Her heart quailed suddenly at the thought and her anger evaporated into deep depression. She had once loved him so much, she would have given her life for him. But never her father's life. From somewhere the thought came to give her strength again. She must do this to avenge her father if for nothing else. Forget everything but that, forget how intimately close they'd been and how gladly she'd given herself to Bruno, forget that he'd taught her how to love and be loved, changing her from virgin to woman and lifting her to the heights of passion and dizzy pleasure along the way. Now all she must remember was watching her father's deepening despair as he wished his life away, and her own hate and bitterness when he died. She must carry that memory with her tomorrow morning and use it to influence the rest of the staff, because that was the only way she could beat Bruno. He was a man ruled by his ambition. She had found that out too late, but at least her experience might help her colleagues now.

CHAPTER TWO

NORRIE arrived at the *Observer* soon after nine the next morning, intending to have a talk with Sue before the meeting started, but when she walked through the main door, she was greeted by one of the women at the desk with, 'I've got a message for you. You're to go to see Mr Denton as soon as you come in.'

The girl eyed her with avid curiosity as Norrie stared at her for a moment, taken by surprise. Then the full implication of the summons hit her; Bruno must have found out about the union meeting and guessed that she'd been talking. So he'd decided to fire her and get her out of the building before she could do him any more damage. Her cheeks slowly suffused with anger as Norrie worked it out and her chin came up defiantly. Well, he needn't think that he could get rid of her that easily. She began to walk towards the staff door, but the girl called her back.

'You're going the wrong way, Mr Denton's taken over the Board Room as his office.'

'Mr Denton,' Norrie said clearly, 'will have to wait. I have more important business to attend to at the moment.' And she went on her way.

Luckily Sue was already in her office and a 'phone call brought Ted hurrying in a few minutes later.

'What's up?' It was Ted's usual greeting, but this morning he looked a bit rattled.

'I want you to take charge of these papers for me,' Norrie told him, handing over her father's battered old briefcase. 'Perhaps you'd better go through them, if you have time before the meeting.'

'Right, I'll do that.' He took the case and then glanced at Norrie's set face. 'You are coming to the meeting, aren't you?'

'I want to—but I might be prevented. Bruno Denton's sent for me and I think he may realise what's happening, so it's quite likely that he'll give me the sack and order me straight out of the building.'

'He can't do that! You're a member of the union. And, besides, he's got no grounds.'

'You don't know him,' Norrie pointed out grimly. 'If he wants to get rid of me, he'll find a way easily enough. I'm only part-time, remember? He could use that as an excuse.'

'But then he'd have to sack all the other part-timers as well,' Sue protested.

'Do you think that would stop him?' Norrie asked forcefully.

They stared at her, only really just beginning to take it in. The 'phone rang stridently in the silence. Sue automatically picked it up and listened, then put the receiver down and said in a numb kind of voice, 'That was the receptionist. It seems that Denton saw you come into the building and he wants to know why you aren't in his office.'

Trust Bruno to take over the Board Room, Norrie thought, recognising the psychological advantage it gave him. She had never even been in there before and her footsteps slowed as she walked along the carpeted corridor towards it. The next few minutes were going to be unpleasant to say the least. Thoughts, memories, chased through her mind but were swiftly buried; there could only be one emotion that must be allowed to show now and that was cold, implacable hatred.

Quickly, before she could change her mind, Norrie knocked on the door and went in, her shoulders braced to face him.

Immediate anti-climax; Bruno was talking on the 'phone, half-sitting on the edge of the big table that took up most of the space in the room. He looked up as she came in and motioned her to sit down in a chair just by the table, but Norrie didn't feel like just sitting there having him watch her while he talked, so she went past the table to the other side of the room. It was an old building and there were long windows looking out over the street with deep wooden sills. Norrie sat on one of the sills and looked out of the window at the bow windowed café across the street and the Cenotaph forming a traffic island in the middle of the square that opened a little further down the road.

Bruno was talking earnestly but she wasn't listening to the words, just the sound of his voice. It brought back long-suppressed memories of other telephone conversations years ago, when each word had been a caress, his voice an extension of his hands to set her body on fire with longing, aching to have him touch her again. Her will-power wasn't strong enough. Inevitably Norrie's eyes turned towards him. He was sitting almost entirely with his back towards her so that she could look at him in safety. He was wearing a conservative dark grey suit but Norrie remembered the broadness of his shoulders beneath it, the muscles in his back and the silky smoothness of his chest when it touched her own. She remembered the athletic slimness of his waist and hips, the flat plane of his stomach, and the proud manhood that had made her his. And she remembered, too, the caged strength of his body, strength over which he had sometimes lost

control during those moments of breathtaking passion
when he had held her in his arms and loved her.

He had finished speaking and she hadn't noticed.
Bruno put down the receiver and paused for a long
moment before slowly turning to face her. His eyes on
her face, he said shortly, 'Stand up.'

Reluctantly Norrie obeyed him, her eyes still dark
and languid from her thoughts, heightened colour on
her cheeks.

For minutes their glances held but then Bruno very
slowly and deliberately lowered his eyes, mentally
stripping her, his gaze scorching her as it lingered in
all the most intimate places.

'Stop it!' Norrie half-turned away from him, looking
at him over her shoulder.

'Stop what?' he asked silkily, his dark eyes only
slowly coming back to her face.

'You know *exactly* what I mean. You were—
undressing me.'

'And weren't you just now indulging in the same
thing?'

'But how did . . .' Norrie stopped, confused and
embarrassed.

'Quite,' Bruno said mockingly.

Norrie bit her lip and took refuge in anger. 'I was
told that you wanted to see me,' she reminded him
coldly.

'Yes, I do.' He came round the table and walked
towards her.

'What—what about?' Norrie's chin was up but she
eyed him warily for all that.

He came close, standing only a foot away. 'Maybe—
to talk about old times.'

Bright sparks of anger flashed in her eyes. 'There's
nothing I want to talk over with you.'

She went to swing away but he caught her hand and held on to it even though she immediately tried to wrench it away.

'It was a long time ago, Norrie. And we meant a lot to each other once.'

Her face flamed. 'How dare you say that? You of all people? All you ever cared about was yourself. You were just using me. Well, I was young then and fool enough to fall for it, but not now.' She laughed scornfully. 'Oh, no. You needn't think you can use me to get what you want a second time.'

Dropping her hand, Bruno moved away to lean against the wall and Norrie felt a momentary sense of relief, but he folded his arms and looked at her rather derisively. 'I thought that by now you'd be adult enough to have looked on the whole thing objectively and thought it through for yourself. I tried to explain my actions to you at the time, but you wouldn't listen. Okay, maybe I didn't manage things as sensitively as I might have done, but don't forget it was my first experience of that kind of thing, and the circumstances were awkward, to say the least. Because of us. Because we were lovers.' He said the word deliberately and Norrie flinched as if he'd struck her, turning away to stare out of the window, her face very pale. After a moment, he went on, 'You listened to everyone else who came running to you with their sob stories, but you wouldn't listen to me. You wouldn't even try to reason it out. You believed them and . . .'

'And I still do,' Norrie cut in bitingly. 'So let's stop wasting time, shall we? You'll never persuade me to change my mind about you, so you may as well go ahead and fire me.'

A withdrawn look, like a shutter being pulled down,

came into Bruno's face. 'Why should I want to fire you?'

'Because it's the only other way you have of trying to keep me quiet about the past—now that you know your first ploy hasn't worked,' Norrie told him with angry triumph in her voice.

Straightening up, Bruno said tiredly, 'I suppose there's no point in trying to convince you that that wasn't my intention in asking you to see me. You won't believe me any more now than you did then.'

'No.'

Bruno rounded on her suddenly, unconcealed anger in his eyes, and for a startled moment Norrie thought that he was going to reach out and grab her, so that she stepped quickly away. But he merely said tersely, 'I have no intention of giving you the sack. If you want to give the people here your version of what happened in Devon, then that's your privilege—and their bad luck. Because you're just going to make things harder for them. I intend to make whatever changes are necessary to make this paper into a going concern, either with the co-operation of the staff or without it. But it would make it a whole lot easier for them if we could do it without a fight.'

'A whole lot easier for you, you mean,' Norrie interrupted scornfully.

To her surprise he nodded. 'And for me,' he agreed. 'But there can only be one winner in this fight, Norrie. Remember that. I'll win in the end. The only people who are going to get hurt are your colleagues—and yourself,' he added deliberately.

Norrie took a deep breath. 'Is that a threat?' she demanded.

Moving to the head of the table he sat down in the Managing Director's chair, leaning back in it casually as if he owned the place. 'I wouldn't dream of threatening you. I haven't forgotten—any more than you have—what we had. And some of what we had was very, very good.'

He said the words silkily, his eyes emphasising his meaning as they ran over her slim body. Norrie flushed and strode across the room to the door, but when she reached it she hesitated and looked back. 'Did you know my father was dead?'

Bruno grew still. 'Yes, I heard. I'm sorry.'

Her hand tightened on the door handle until it hurt. 'He died because of you. Because of what you did to him. I'll never forgive you for that.' And then she stepped out of the room, walking blindly down the corridor and breaking into a run as she reached the stairs.

Sue and Ted were waiting for her in Sue's office. They looked up anxiously when she hurried in. 'What happened?' Sue demanded. 'Did you get kicked out?'

Somehow Norrie brought her whirling thoughts back to the present and shook her head. 'No. But—but he warned me off. Said that raking up the past wouldn't do any good. That we'd lose.' Her voice trailed off.

'Are you all right? Did he upset you?' Sue asked with frowning concern.

'Oh, no. I'm okay.' Norrie tried to pull herself together. 'Having to face him brought it all back, that's all.'

'What else did he say?' Ted demanded.

'He said that if we fought him, we'd be the only losers. Because he'd win in the end.'

'Oh, did he?' Ted bristled. 'We'll see about that. I'd better go,' he added, after glancing at his watch. 'See you girls at the meeting.'

When he'd gone Sue fished a half bottle of whisky and a couple of glasses out of the bottom drawer of her desk. 'Here,' she offered, half-filling the glasses, 'you look as if you need this. Give yourself a bit of Dutch courage before you have to get up and face them all.'

Norrie laughed hollowly. 'Facing everyone here is nothing after ten minutes with Bruno.'

'I take it,' Sue said carefully, 'that you knew him pretty well?'

'I suppose you could say that,' Norrie admitted. The neat whisky felt raw on her tongue but warm inside. She was surprised to see that her hand was shaking a little and was annoyed that she'd let Bruno get to her that much. 'He was down in Devon for nearly five months and came to the paper every day.'

'He couldn't have been that old then, could he? He only looks about thirty now.'

'Thirty-two,' Norrie corrected. 'He was about twenty-seven then.'

'Quite young for that kind of job, surely?'

Norrie drained her glass. 'He was old enough. Quite old enough to know what he wanted and how to get it.'

'And if you knew him that well, he must have wanted you—and got you, too.'

Norrie looked at Sue and nodded briefly, then stood up. 'It must be time for the meeting, let's go, shall we?'

The entire staff of the *Welford Observer* without exception attended the union meeting held in the big office on the ground floor. The main doors were closed and the 'phones switched off so that there wouldn't be any interruptions. Ted climbed on to a box and addressed everyone first, explaining about the take-over and saying that changes were bound to be made, but that he'd got some evidence about the way they might be handled that he wanted them all to hear. But before he could call Norrie forward, Harry Simons, the Editor, demanded to speak.

Taking Ted's place on the box, he said, 'All of you have already had a letter about this, explaining the position. It's early days yet and there's no point in rushing into precipitate and possibly unnecessary action before we even know what's going to happen. By now most of you have met Mr Denton from Provincial Press. He seems to be a fair-minded man whose aim is to get the paper back on its feet, and not necessarily by cutting back on staff.'

'Fair-minded?' Ted Burtenshaw broke in loudly. 'I'd not call what he did at Norrie's old paper fair-minded. You listen to this.' He pulled Norrie forward. 'Go on, girl, you tell 'em.'

The Editor grudgingly gave up his place to her and Norrie looked nervously round, clutching her briefcase tightly to her. For a few seconds she couldn't speak but then she remembered the people who had trusted Bruno all those years ago and her voice came out firm and clear as, for the third time in two days, she described the way he'd got that other paper 'back on its feet'. 'Denton was given a *carte blanche* by his company and he took full advantage of it,' she told them. 'He used underhand methods to find out the weaknesses of the senior members of the staff and, if they wouldn't agree to put through the changes he wanted, he used those weaknesses either as a threat or to get rid of them. He even went as far as to suggest absolutely outrageous changes knowing that they wouldn't be tolerated, which gave him an excuse to get rid of people he wanted out of the way. I have here several written statements from staff of the *Westland Gazette* that Denton sacked. They detail his ruthlessness and cruelty.' She looked questioningly at Ted. 'Shall I read them out, or would you rather?'

'No, no. You go ahead, girl.'

Norrie read them carefully and clearly, concentrating on what she was doing, but her voice faltered and dried up completely as she turned a page and caught sight of Bruno standing in a corner near the door. He hadn't been there when the meeting had started and she hadn't seen him come in so had no idea how long he'd been listening. As her voice died away everyone in the room followed her eyes and turned to look, many of them with angry scowls on their faces when they saw who it was. Bruno stood their scrutiny quite calmly, leaning against the wall with his arms folded, waiting for her to go on.

After a few moments Norrie did so, but her voice was unsteady now, and no one was really listening. She came to a finish and looked at Ted. He stepped forward.

'I think we all owe Norrie a vote of thanks for bringing this to our attention.' There was a general cheer and loud clapping as Norrie got down; many people again turning round to see how Bruno was taking it, but his face betrayed no emotion whatsoever. Ted went on, 'Well, you've all heard what we can expect. The facts speak for themselves and I for one think we should . . .'

'One moment.' Bruno's voice cut through the murmur of approval at Ted's words like a knife and there was instant silence in the big room. 'You have heard a great many accusations made at me this morning, and I think it only fair that I should be allowed to answer them. Or am I to be condemned out of hand?' he added, when Ted stood silent.

Everyone began to speak to their neighbour but the

buzz turned to speculation as Ted said, 'All right, we'll hear what you've got to say,' and Bruno made his way through the crowded room to the makeshift rostrum, but he didn't stand on it, he was tall enough for them all to see him.

'Thank you.' Bruno turned to face them all, his hands casually in the pockets of his trousers. He looked very much in control of himself, supremely self-confident, and Norrie suddenly felt sick inside, knowing his power to charm, to sway people the way he wanted. 'Miss Peters,' he began, nodding in her direction, 'has given you a lot of evidence about the *Westland Gazette* which sounds very damning.' He paused. 'On the face of it. But consider, if you will, the circumstances. That was a very rural newspaper that had been run without change for over a hundred years. Things had been good once so why change them? The senior staff were, to say the least, very senior, and very much against change. The circulation of the paper had gone right down and there were others in the wings just waiting to move in and finish it altogether. They were digging their own graves but were too blind to see it.

'I spent several months there trying to reason with them, to make them see that they must get into the twentieth century fast or go under completely. But hardly any of the senior staff would listen. They were too stuck in their ways. Then I got a rocket from my own bosses; they'd already given me more time than they'd intended. So then the ruthlessness and cruelty that Miss Peters has described to you comes into it. I admit that I was ruthless. Even cruel, if you can call it cruel to tell a man that he must change or go. Some of them I think would have agreed if it hadn't been for the attitude of the Editor, Miss Peters' father.'

Norrie kept her head down but she felt everyone stir and look at her, and a whisper go round the room.

'He refused point blank to improve or change the paper in any way and bullied—or encouraged, if you like—his colleagues to do the same. And so they had to go. Much as I regretted the decision, I had no choice but to fire them.' Bruno paused to let that sink in, then went on, 'You have heard the statements from these people for yourselves, but what are they, when it boils down to it, but the complaints of people who have been made redundant after being in their jobs for a great many years. Miss Peters has accused me of cruelty, but doesn't everyone who has been made redundant consider that they have been treated cruelly—by their bosses, by the Government, by fate? But most of these people from the *Westland Gazette* brought it on themselves by their dog-in-the-manger attitudes. They have only themselves to blame. The *Gazette*, as anyone here can find out for themselves, is now a flourishing newspaper with a wide circulation that is rapidly expanding and showing a nice margin of profit.'

Bruno deliberately paused again, then said forcefully, 'As I intend that the *Welford Observer* shall show a profit. At the moment this paper is headed on the same downward spiral as the *Gazette*, but for different reasons. There, it was the staff that was behind the times, here it is mostly the plant and the format. Yes, there will be changes here, you can be sure of that. But not necessarily sweeping economies, although some will be made in certain departments. In fact I intend to invest a great deal of capital into the paper so that we can get rid of that antiquated machinery which you know as well as I do is completely out of date. And if you're thinking that

modern machinery will require less manpower in
that department, I'll tell you now that I intend to
print a mid-week edition of the paper that will be
distributed free to every household in the district.
Hopefully this will attract a good deal more revenue
in advertisements, another aspect of the paper that I
intend to concentrate on.' He gave them time to take
that in, then said emphatically, 'The *Observer* *must*
be made to pay. And it's going to take the hard
work of all of us to do that. Remember that all of us
here *are* the *Observer*. We're a team and must pull
together, not against one another. I need your help;
I can't do it alone. And I hope you'll give it to me.'
He looked round at the sea of eyes and gave them
one of his charming grins. 'I've talked for so long I
could even drink a cup of that terrible coffee from
the vending machine—which is one of the first
things we're going to improve on.'

There was a general sound of endorsing laughter as
Bruno moved to turn away, but Norrie stepped
forward and said quickly, 'Just a moment.'

Bruno's face hardened as he recognised her voice
and turned to face her. 'Yes?'

Norrie's chin came up defiantly and she made sure
her voice carried to all corners of the big room.
'You've told us a great deal that *sounds* very
encouraging, Mr Denton,' she said with heavy
sarcasm. 'But can you guarantee that no one here will
lose their jobs?'

For a moment Bruno just looked at her without
answering, an angry gleam in his dark eyes, then he
said quite steadily, 'No, Miss Peters, I cannot. If I
think that someone is below standard, not pulling their
weight, or being particularly bloody-minded, then that
person will have to go.'

'Thank you,' Norrie said triumphantly into the shocked silence. 'That's all I wanted to know.'

Bruno looked at her for a moment longer before giving a curt nod, then strode out of the room.

There was silence for a minute as he went out of the office and then uproar as everybody started talking at once. Both Ted and Sue turned to Norrie and spoke excitedly but she didn't hear them. Although no one else in the room knew it, that last glance that she and Bruno had exchanged had been a tacit declaration of war. He knew that she was going to fight him to the bitter end, and she had no doubt that he would do the same. She shivered suddenly, as if someone had walked over her grave, and looked at Sue rather dazedly as she said, 'Good for you, Norrie. You really floored him with that last question.'

'That's as maybe,' Ted reminded them warningly. 'But if he is going to put money into the paper that will carry a lot of weight. We've been crying out for new machinery for years. And this idea of a free mid-week paper is a good one, you can't deny that.'

Norrie looked at Ted in some dismay, realising that Bruno's new ideas and his power of persuasion had half won him over already. 'Modern machinery needs less people to run it,' she pointed out tartly. 'You're not going to just wait around and see who he's going to get rid of, are you?'

'No, we need to get an undertaking from Denton now that he won't make anyone redundant,' Sue insisted.

Ted got back up on his box, called for order and eventually managed to get it, but the meeting went on for a good hour afterwards before it was agreed that Ted and a couple of other union representatives would ask for a further meeting with Bruno to find out

exactly what he was going to do, what staff alterations
he was going to make, and whether he was going to ask
for any voluntary redundancies. Norrie was hoping for
something more active but was pleased that they were
at least doing *something*. They were forewarned and
could put up a fight. Someone suggested that she
should be one of the representatives but she hastily
refused; stirring everyone up to oppose Bruno was one
thing, having to face him again was quite another.

Not a lot of work was done at the *Observer* that day.
Everyone was discussing the union meeting and airing
their own views on what should have been done or
said. Norrie went back to Sue's office feeling mentally
exhausted, the high adrenalin all drained away, and
she was glad to sit and let the talk wash over her for a
while. But then she remembered that Ben was with the
baby-minder and the woman charged by the hour so
she hastily said goodbye and dashed off. It was nearly
lunch-time and the main road through the town was
heavy with traffic; Norrie had to wait at the crossing
outside the *Observer* office for several impatient
minutes before she could get across. As she waited she
had the peculiar feeling that she was being watched,
but it wasn't until she got to the other side that she
remembered that Bruno had seen her come into the
building. Stepping on to the pavement, she let the
crowd go round her and turned to look back. Bruno
was standing at the window of the Board Room,
watching her. For several moments their eyes held,
but then he lifted a hand in a mocking salute and
Norrie quickly turned and walked rapidly away.

Over the weekend, Norrie worked on a couple of
features that she'd had in mind for some time and that
didn't need too much research, but she found it
difficult to keep her mind on her work. Her thoughts

kept drifting back to Bruno and the colossal row
they'd had after he'd sacked her father. She had been
almost hysterically furious, hurling abuse at him,
unable to take it in that the man she loved had
betrayed her in this way. Bruno had been quite cool
and had tried to reason with her at first, but then he,
too, had been goaded into emotional anger, telling her
to grow up and face reality. They had said some really
hurtful things to each other then; she had even lied
and called him a lousy lover because she knew that
would hurt him most. He had looked murderous and
she thought he was going to hit her, but instead he had
become icy cold and withdrawn, saying bitingly,
'You're behaving like a spoilt, hysterical teenager. I
want a woman not a child. When you come to your
senses and realise that you're an individual and not
Daddy's little girl any more, call me.' And then he'd
walked out on her yelled insults. Within two weeks
he'd appointed a new editor and left the town. Norrie
hadn't seen him because she'd taken her father away
for a holiday to try and help him get over it, not that it
had done any good at all, if anything he was even more
bitter and miserable. When they got back she'd found
a letter from Bruno waiting for her, but she'd still
been so angry that she'd torn it through without
opening it and burnt the remains. He hadn't written
again and she hadn't expected him to; Bruno wasn't
the type to take a second rebuff.

Taking the easy way out, Norrie posted the two
feature articles off to Sue and didn't go into the office
again until Wednesday. Already changes were being
made; the reception area was being redecorated and
modernised with a built-in counter instead of the two
old desks. 'And there's going to be easy chairs and a
low table where customers can sit and discuss what

they want with us,' one of the girls explained excitedly. 'We're going to have a whole new image.'

Sue, too, was busy. 'We're probably going to need to have at least one more feature every week especially for the new mid-week edition,' she told Norrie happily. 'Probably with the emphasis on some feature within the area. Can you take on any more work, Norrie, or are your hands full with Ben?'

'Yes, of course I can. I have too much spare time,' Norrie admitted. 'And Ben's going to nursery school every morning next term which will help.'

'Good.' Sue put the end of her pen in her mouth and chewed it reflectively. 'Of course you're still restricted to using public transport. It would help if you had a car, you know. You could get all around the area then, not just in the town.'

'I've managed okay without one so far. Taking on a little more work would hardly cover the expense of a car, Sue.'

'No, I suppose not. Still . . .'

'Was it Bruno Denton's idea that I'd be more useful if I had a car?' Norrie demanded.

'What? Oh no, it was mine. He just suggested that our features could now cover a wider area.'

'So you've been talking to him?'

'Yes.' Sue looked at her a little awkwardly. 'I know that in your eyes he's a louse, but honestly, Norrie, he does have some really good ideas. For instance, he . . .'

'Not just in my eyes,' Norrie interrupted tartly. 'What about all the people he's sacked in his time?' She leaned forward, saying urgently, 'Can't you see what he's doing? He's trying to charm you into being on his side. And succeeding, too, by the sound of it. That's his way, Sue. He'll butter you up with talk of more features, make you feel important, possibly even hint at a rise, and you'll probably be okay as long as you go along with him, but if you want to do things your way instead of his—then you'll be in for a nasty shock. Opposing Bruno Denton is what he calls sheer bloody-mindedness. Remember?'

Sue looked at her and gave a puzzled shake of her head. 'I honestly don't know what to believe any more. He certainly seems okay on the surface, but if what you say is true ... Perhaps he's changed since you knew him,' she suggested hopefully.

Norrie shook her head emphatically. 'Why should he? I can't see it. What happened when the union delegates went to see him?'

'Bruno said that he didn't envisage having to make any staff cuts but he assured them that if he had to he would call for voluntary redundancies first and that full payments and compensation would be paid. And you know, Norrie, there are a couple of men in the linotype room who are nearly sixty and would be glad to take early retirement.'

Norrie saw all right; Sue's use of Bruno's Christian name told her that the other girl had completely changed sides since she'd seen her last. One talk with Bruno and he had Sue eating out of his hand, she thought bitterly. For a startled moment she wondered if Bruno would use the same tactics here as he had in Devon and become Sue's lover to get the inside information he wanted on the staff of the *Observer*; the kind of information that doesn't appear in the Personnel records but all your workmates know; whether a man drinks too much, if a marriage is breaking up, who's having an affair with whom. The kind of gossip that could be used as moral blackmail when Bruno wanted to get his own way. But the thought of Sue and Bruno together was more than

Norrie could take and she quickly changed the subject, handing over her work and asking for her next assignment.

'I thought we might do an article on that shell grotto over in Radbury. It's falling into decay, evidently, and some publicity might ginger up the local council or historical society to take it over and try to preserve it.'

'Whereabouts in Radbury is it? I've never even heard of the place,' Norrie admitted.

'I'm not surprised. It isn't open to the public or anything. It's actually a series of underground rooms. Some eccentric millionaire had them built in his garden in the nineteenth century on the lines of the Hell Fire Caves in High Wycombe. There's a meeting-room and a robing-room, that kind of thing. And every room is lined with patterns made out of sea-shells and bits of marble, from what I can gather. I seem to remember that there's just one old man who keeps an eye on the place; stops the vandals and courting couples from getting in there. If you ask around in the village someone's bound to know who he is.'

'Okay. When do you want it?'

'Next week, if you can. Oh, and try and find out when we can send a photographer round, will you?'

When Norrie left Sue she stood in the corridor indecisively for a few seconds, then made her way to the linotype room. Ted Burtenshaw was okay, but there were several younger, more left wing men who also worked there. She managed to beckon one of them over without attracting anyone else's attention and confided her worries to him. 'Isn't there anything we can do, Dave?' she asked.

'You know what they're like here; won't move a

muscle until you put a bomb under them. And anyway, they don't think they've got anything to protest about.'

'And they won't have until it's too late to do anything about it. Did they get the assurances from the new management in writing?'

'No, they just took Denton's word for it. Ted said he felt we could trust him.'

'Oh Lord, not Ted too! I thought he had more sense.'

'Tell you what I'll do,' Dave offered. 'I'll get in touch with union headquarters, and maybe I'll do a bit of printing on my own account. That might stir things up a bit.'

'Great. Let me know if I can help,' Norrie enthused.

Dave slipped an arm round her waist. 'How about coming out for a drink tonight to talk it over?'

Norrie moved neatly away from him. 'Shame on you, and you a married man.'

He gave a leering grin. 'What difference does that make? You're not the kind of girl to let a little thing like that get in the way, now are you? You've been around.'

'Goodbye, Dave.' Norrie walked away and left him, realising, by no means for the first time, that looking after a toddler who not only bore your surname but also looked like you, could have more disadvantages than the obvious ones. But it had been worth it to try and get something moving. Dave disliked capitalism almost as much as she disliked Bruno and would get far more notice taken of him at headquarters than she ever would if she'd gone there.

She spent most of that afternoon on the telephone, trying to find out the name of the man who looked after the grotto at Radbury, and eventually tracked him down via the local vicar, the sexton, the village shop and a neighbour who obligingly went along to the old man's house to fetch him. He turned out to be a bit deaf and the call turned into a three-sided conversation with the neighbour talking to Norrie and then shouting in the old man's ear. They arranged, after about ten minutes of explanation, for Norrie to go over to see the caves the next morning, and she then 'phoned Sue to ask if the photographer was free.

'Just a minute, I'll check. I'm glad you managed to find him, the grotto should make an interesting feature.' Norrie heard a man's voice in the background while she waited and then Sue explaining about the feature before breaking off to speak on the internal phone. 'He can't make it tomorrow, Norrie,' she came back. 'He'll have to go some other time. Let him have the details, will you?'

'All right, I'll drop them in tomorrow on my way back.'

'What time are you going?'

'There's a bus just after nine; I'll get that.' But she thought it better not to mention that the bus only went to the large village near Radbury and that she would have to walk the last two miles. Buses only went directly to the little village twice a day at seven-thirty in the morning and five-thirty in the evening, to collect and take home people who worked in the town. Norrie owned a bicycle and thought of taking that, but Radbury was at least thirteen miles away and she remembered one extremely steep hill that completely put her off the idea.

Ben got dropped off at the nursery school as early as she could the next morning and then Norrie ran into the town square to catch the bus. It was already there and a few people were starting to get on, although there wasn't much of a queue at this time in the morning. As she sprinted across the square she was startled by the sound of a car horn close by so she stopped and looked round, thinking that she was about to be run down. But the only car around was a gold-coloured Jaguar sports car parked on the kerb. As she looked towards it the horn sounded again and she saw Bruno in the driving seat. Opening the window, he called out, 'I'm going your way; I'll give you a lift.'

For a moment Norrie was too surprised to think, but then she glanced at the bus and saw the last person about to get on. 'But I'm not going *your* way,' she yelled back at him, and ran across to the bus, slipping through the doors just before they closed.

' 'Ere, you were cutting that a bit fine, weren't you?' the driver said in surprised admiration. 'Could have got yourself stuck, you could.'

Norrie grinned at him, paying for her ticket and taking a seat half way along the almost empty bus. As it pulled away she looked out of the window, expecting to see Bruno drive off, but he fell in behind the bus, following it through the one-way system around the town. Norrie's heart skipped a couple of beats and she breathed a sigh of relief when they reached the main road and the gold car accelerated past.

It wasn't until then that she began to wonder how he'd known where she was going and why he had bothered to offer her a lift anyway. The first he could have learnt from Sue presumably, but the second . . . that was completely baffling.

The weather was quite bright and, as always, it gave her pleasure to drive through the countryside, to see the patchwork of crops growing in the fields, ranging from dark green to the bright yellow of mustard seed.

It wasn't as scenically picturesque as her native Devon, but it would do, it would most certainly do. The bus took a meandering route through a dozen little villages, dropping off parcels and passengers along the way and going so slowly that Norrie looked anxiously at her watch; at this rate she would only have about an hour at the grotto before it would be time to get the bus back. Eventually it reached the terminus and Norrie got out with the last three passengers. She had been given directions and knew which way to go but when she turned to walk to her left she stopped precipitately. The gold Jaguar was parked nearby and Bruno was leaning against it, smoking a cigarette and looking as if he had all the time in the world.

When he saw her he looked at his watch. 'I could have saved you over half an hour.'

Biting her lip, Norrie answered shortly, 'Time isn't everything.' And went to walk past him.

But as she came up to him, Bruno said, 'Are you going to get in the car or do I follow you while you walk all the way to Radbury?'

'That would be very stupid.'

'It would indeed,' he agreed.

'So why don't you just go away and leave me alone. I have no intention of going anywhere with you,' she said, moving away.

'But you will.'

Again she came to a stop and faced him, bright sparks of anger in her eyes. 'What gives you that idea?'

'Because you dislike looking silly as much as the next person, and you'll look extremely silly walking along with your nose in the air and me driving alongside you.'

'You wouldn't dare!'

A gleam that she remembered of old came into

Bruno's eyes. 'Wouldn't I?' He opened the car door. 'Well, which is it to be?'

'You can go to hell!' But some women had come out of a nearby shop and were looking at them curiously. Norrie suddenly had a mental picture of what they would look like going down the road. And Bruno would do it, too. 'Damn you,' she swore at him forcefully, but stepped forward and got into the car.

Bruno shut the door and then came round to get in beside her. Norrie caught the tang of his aftershave and was aware of his size and the self-confident masculinity that he exuded at every pore and suddenly she felt like a fly caught in a web, who is too mesmerised to run when the spider comes towards her.

CHAPTER THREE

TAKING refuge in attack, Norrie demanded curtly, 'Why have you followed me here?'

'Lots of reasons,' Bruno answered calmly, as he started the engine and began to drive away. 'The sun is shining, I felt like a few hours away from the office, I'm interested in the grotto you're going to see.' He paused and glanced at her. 'And I thought that perhaps we could have a talk, renew an old friendship.'

'Friendship is the last thing I feel for you.'

'All right, renew an old enmity, then.'

'That's ridiculous,' Norrie said scornfully. 'The less one sees of an enemy the better.'

'Oh, I don't know, I think you're quite enjoying hating me. You're certainly enjoying trying to get everyone at the *Observer* riled up against me.'

'And there's the real reason why you followed me; you want to try and talk me round again,' she accused him. 'But you should know by now that you're wasting your time.' She spoke belligerently, wanting him to know how much she disliked him, but as a protection, too, against her basic reaction to his nearness. It was all there still, the masculinity and strength that had so overpowered her the first time, the chemistry that had drawn them inexorably into bed together. She had been lost then, so drowned in her love for him that she'd been blind to everything else until it had been too late. But now she must be on her guard, must never let her barrier of hatred waver for a second.

Bruno didn't speak for a moment as he overtook a tractor that had been blocking their way for some time, but then he smiled rather sardonically. 'You know something, Norrie, you have a very exaggerated idea of your powers of persuasion. The people at the *Observer* aren't stupid; they're not going to commit themselves one way or the other until they see what's in it for them. It would be pretty silly to try and fight me when they're going to do well out of the take-over. Which way?' he added as they came to a junction.

'To the left. There should be a sign about a hundred yards along.' She would have liked to continue the argument but the old man who looked after the grotto was sitting on a chair under the sign, smoking a pipe as he waited for Norrie to arrive. 'Thought you were going to walk here, missie,' he observed as Norrie shook hands with him.

'I was but this—er—gentleman offered me a lift,' Norrie told him on a sarcastic note that wasn't lost on Bruno. 'He's the new proprietor of the *Welford Observer*, Bruno Denton.'

'Folks call me Sid,' the old man offered. 'The caves are this way.' He unlocked a barred metal gate in the wall behind him and led them down an overgrown path shaded by tall rhododendron bushes that were a mass of mauve and pink flowers. The earth beneath their feet was damp, never touched by the sun, and gave off a sweet, pungent smell as they disturbed it.

'Who does this ground belong to?' Norrie asked him.

'It was part of the grounds of the manor once—you won't see it, it's about a quarter of a mile away—but when the squire got killed in the first world war, his widow sold most of the agricultural land off to farmers, but she gave the caves to the parish, to be looked after by the parish council. Although I don't know what she thought they would use them for.' The man laughed richly, enjoying the thought, and it was impossible not to smile with him.

The shrubs cleared a little and they saw a thick wooden door set into what looked like a large mound of earth, rather like the entrance to an underground fall-out shelter. Sid selected another key. 'Have you brought a torch?' he demanded.

'Why no. Isn't there any electricity laid on?'

'No. Electricity would spoil it. Never mind, I keep a few candles inside.' Opening the door, he displayed a little cubbyhole with a stool and narrow shelf. 'This is where I sit to take the money on open days. Not that there's many as comes here now. It's too hard to find, even if they know about it.' There was a box of candles on the shelf and Sid selected two, fiddling in his pocket for his matches, but Bruno produced his lighter.

Giving one of the candles to Bruno, Sid led the way down the narrow corridor into the caves with Norrie following him and Bruno coming last. Her first impression was one of dankness and Norrie shivered, feeling suddenly cold. The candles' light showed white walls on which graffiti had been scrawled in places, hearts and names mostly, with here and there the name of a football team. As if it was his fault, Sid said in apology, 'It's the youngsters that do it. I try to watch them but I have to sit at the door and take the money, then there's always some fool whose candle goes out and I have to go and find them.'

The corridor opened into a domed room and Sid held his candle high so that they could see the ornate shellwork which patterned the roof and most of the walls. Most of the decoration was still intact but it had fallen off in places, especially lower down where people could reach it. 'This was the Robing Room,' Sid told them and when they'd looked round led them on to other chambers, equally ornate, until Norrie had completely lost her sense of direction.

'Is there a map of the lay-out?' Norrie asked the old man.

'I've got one pinned up by the main door. I'll do you a copy, if you like.'

'Thanks, but just a rough sketch with the names of the rooms would do.'

'Perhaps Sid could do that for you now,' Bruno suggested smoothly, 'while we take another look round.'

'Oh, but . . .'

'Right-oh.' Sid, ever helpful, was off before she could stop him, the light from his candle receding down the corridor and cutting off abruptly as he turned a corner.

'Was that necessary?' Norrie demanded sharply. 'It could have waited, surely?'

'I know.' He said it softly but immediately tension filled the underground chamber, seeming to bounce back from the walls, loud in the silence.

Filled with sudden fear, Norrie turned to hurry after Sid, but Bruno put out an arm to stop her. She hit out at him in blind panic. 'Get out of my way. Don't come near me.'

'Why? What are you so afraid of?' Bruno tried to catch hold of her hand but she jerked it out of the way, knocking his arm and sending the candle flying from his hold. It went out before it hit the ground, leaving them in total darkness.

Norrie gasped and instinctively put her arms out in front of her, but all she touched was Bruno's jacket.

Before she could move away, he caught hold of her hands. 'Are you afraid of the dark?'

'No. No, of course not.' She tried to pull her hands away but he held them fast.

'And you're surely not afraid of me. After all, you've been alone with me in the dark many times.'

'Which is something I prefer to forget,' Norrie assured him, but her throat constricted as she said it. 'Will you please let go of my hands?'

'Why? So that you can run away again?' he asked sardonically. Then, abruptly, 'Why didn't you answer my letter?'

'I should have thought that was obvious,' she retorted. 'Look, this is ridiculous, just standing here. If we call out to Sid he'll come and find us.'

'And be one of the fools he talked about?' Bruno mocked.

'It was an accident.'

'Was it? How's Sid to know that? He may think we want to be in the dark together.' And he drew Norrie nearer to him.

'Let go of me.' Her voice rose in alarm. 'Damn you, Bruno, I suppose you think this is funny. Well, I don't.' She opened her mouth to call Sid but felt Bruno's hand moving up her arm and then it was in her hair, his other hand going to her waist as he pulled her against him. 'Don't!' Agitatedly she put her hands on his chest and tried to push him away, but his grip tightened and his mouth sought hers, finding her cheek as she tried to turn her head. His lips moved across her skin, featherlight, and Norrie swore at him as she felt them touch the corner of her mouth. 'No! Don't.' The words came out on a panic-stricken gasp, lost under his mouth as Bruno's lips closed firmly over hers.

Norrie struggled wildly, her body squirming in his hold, but he held her tightly and there was no way she could move her head. She tried to knee him, but he bent her back so that if she tried it again she would lose her balance. Thwarted, Norrie tried to bite his lips but Bruno forced her mouth open, hurting her in his domination, so that she could only make sounds of furious anger in her throat. The darkness seemed to close about them, making it all the worse because she couldn't see him, could only feel his lips, his hands holding her and the strong hardness of his body as he arched her under him. Bringing up her right hand, Norrie raked it across his face and felt a stab of satisfaction when he flinched and released her mouth. 'You little bitch,' he muttered under his breath, and then took her mouth again without mercy, his lips ravishing hers greedily, making her head swim and her body tremble.

It was a sensation Norrie hadn't felt for a long time; the sheer shock of memory made her stop resisting and stand still in his embrace, the fire that he had always been able to light in her beginning to rise from the embers that she had thought long since dead and cold. In an agony of revulsion at her body's betrayal, Norrie made a supreme effort and pushed herself violently away from him, so violently that she fell back and was only saved from falling by the wall. The sound of Bruno's breathing was heavy in the darkness and Norrie was afraid that he would reach for her again, but after a few moments he snapped on his lighter and moved closer so that he could see her face by its light.

Norrie leant back against the wall, feeling its cold and dampness through her clothes. 'I hate you,' she stammered wildly. 'God, how I hate you. You just had to do that, didn't you? What's the matter—can't you take the fact that a woman you've had is capable of resisting you?' she asked with fierce derisiveness. 'Well, this one certainly is. You leave me cold.'

It was as if he hadn't heard. Bruno continued to look at her in silence, only moving when they heard the sound of Sid's footsteps echoing along the corridor, then he turned to look for the candle, found it and relit it. Then he said in a strange kind of voice, 'I was merely trying to prove something to myself.'

'And did you?'

He gave a cold, mirthless laugh. 'Oh, yes. I most certainly did.'

'What did you prove?' The words were torn from her even though she hadn't wanted to ask them.

This time his laugh was mocking as it echoed round the cavern. 'Why, what I suspected all along, of course.'

And that, Norrie knew, was all she was going to get out of him. 'You sod,' she swore at him. 'Why the hell did you have to come here?'

Bruno's face hardened, but Sid came into the cave just then and Norrie turned to him in relief, needing now to get out into the open air again; the walls of the underground rooms and the darkness had become more than oppressive, they seemed to be closing in on her from every side. 'I think I've seen enough. Let's go outside, shall we?'

Once out of the caves Norrie became professionally efficient, getting out her notebook and asking Sid all he knew about the grotto. After a few minutes Bruno wandered off by himself, pushing his way through the shrubs that barred another path further into the garden. Sid was a nice old man and enjoyed having someone to talk to about his favourite subject, Norrie didn't want to be abrupt but his meandering answers to her questions enabled her mind to go back to that nasty scene in the cave and she didn't want to think of that, so she tried to keep him to the point without offending him. He accepted her briskness resignedly; the old who had little time left giving way to the pressure of the young who think they have no time at all.

When Bruno came back she was arranging for a photographer to come the following week. Sid escorted them to the gate and waved goodbye as they drove away, a smile on his face at the thought of having his photo in the paper.

As soon as they'd turned the corner Norrie took out her pad again and went through her notes, making an addition here and there while her memory was fresh. Bruno glanced at what she was doing and then kept his eyes on the road, concentrating on negotiating the narrow, twisting lanes. Norrie hung it out for as long as she could, but eventually had to close the pad and put it away in her handbag, and then there was nothing to do but look fixedly out of the windows and try and pretend that Bruno wasn't there. Which was pretty difficult one way and another.

It was he who broke the taut silence. 'Old Sid's quite a character.'

'Yes,' she answered unhelpfully.

'But then I suppose you get quite a few characters around here?'

'Yes.'

'So why don't you do a feature on them, or perhaps a series of short features?'

Norrie saw instantly that it was a good idea; every village had its own eccentric from retired snake dancer to daffodil eater, and it would sell papers to the whole village when they knew one of their own was being

featured. But she wasn't going to let Bruno know that.
'It's hardly a new idea,' she answered dampeningly. 'It
was probably done ages ago.'

'Don't you know?'

'I've only been on the staff for a couple of years.'

'Well, it could be worth checking. And village
populations change; it might be worth bringing it up
to date.'

Norrie made a dismissive sound. 'Tell Sue you want
it done, if you're that keen.'

'Can't you suggest it to her?'

'It's *your* idea,' Norrie pointed out disparagingly.
'And Sue's my boss; she tells me what to do.'

'Aren't you allowed to have any ideas of your own?'

'Sometimes,' she admitted grudgingly.

'But you don't intend to make use of the idea I've
given you simply because it came from me, is that it?'
He waited but when she didn't answer, added
sarcastically, 'You know, Norrie, you should never let
your emotions interfere with business.'

She turned to glare at him, grey eyes flashing
angrily. 'Well, that's certainly something you could
never be accused of.'

'On the contrary,' Bruno replied acidly, 'I once let
emotion get in the way and almost lost my job over it.
So I learned my lesson the hard way and it's one
mistake I don't intend to repeat.'

Impossible not to know that he was referring to
their affair, but it was hardly how Norrie remembered
the circumstances. And she didn't believe for a minute
that he had almost lost his job; he was far too
ruthlessly efficient for that. But she was curious and
said, 'I'm sure you needn't worry about losing your
job this time—although I notice you are working for a
different company now. Westland Holdings didn't

have the sense to see you for what you were and kick you out, did they?'

'Sorry to disappoint you; I left on my own account.'

'To become a bigger fish in Provincial Press, I suppose,' Norrie remarked sneeringly.

Bruno looked at her with a twisted grin. 'Thinking of trying to do me some harm there? What a nasty little mind you have. But I'm afraid it won't do you any good.' He changed to a lower gear as they went round the roundabout on the outskirts of Welford.

'Why not? Maybe there are some things in your past you've been careful to keep from them that they might be interested to hear about,' Norrie threatened smoothly.

'In that case you'd better let them know. Why don't you write to the Managing Director?'

'Maybe I'll do just that,' she retorted, thinking that he was trying to call her bluff. 'What's his name?'

Bruno grinned and glanced towards her. 'It's Denton. Bruno Denton. The company's mine; I formed it over three years ago.'

Norrie could have hit him, but had to bite her lip and try and contain her anger. He had scored a hit, but letting him see her chagrin would only increase his enjoyment.

The traffic was thicker as they entered the town and Bruno slowed down. 'Are you going back to the office? Shall I drop you there?'

Glancing at her watch, Norrie saw that it was twenty to twelve. 'No, the next corner would be better, by the Post Office.' There was a 'phone box there and she would be able to 'phone the child-minder and tell her she needn't meet Ben at the nursery school after all.

Noticing her action, he said casually, 'Do you live near there?'

'No, but I want to 'phone someone.'

'A boyfriend?'

Norrie looked at him and wanted to hurt, to get her own back for that kiss in the grotto. 'It's to arrange to meet the person I live with,' she said tauntingly. 'I suppose I ought to thank you; your giving me a lift means that I'll be able to have lunch with him after all.'

She was disappointed. Bruno's eyebrows flickered but he betrayed no other sign of emotion. They came to the corner and he pulled up and turned to face her. 'I hope he looks after you.'

'Oh, he does—beautifully.' She said it sensuously, her lips pouting, letting him assume that she was referring to sex.

'I'm glad to hear it,' he replied smoothly. 'I hope for his sake he knows how to handle your temper—as well as your body,' he added, his eyes running insolently over her.

Norrie nearly lost her temper then, but managed to stay cool and say, 'He's more than adequate in all departments. Compared with him you're way down the league.'

To her annoyance he merely laughed. 'Have a good lunch.'

'On second thoughts,' Norrie snapped, 'I'm not going to thank you for the lift. After all I didn't ask for it and I would certainly rather have been alone.' And she got quickly out of the car.

As a parting shot it wasn't much, but it made her feel a little better as she went into the Post Office, careful not to let Bruno have the satisfaction of seeing her look back.

But the lift had saved her both time and money because she was able to catch the baby-minder just before she set out to collect Ben. As she walked along to the nursery Norrie tried to think about her article on the grotto, but it was impossible to keep her mind away from Bruno. Why had he kissed her like that, so fiercely, so mercilessly? Why had he kissed her at all? Surely even he wasn't so egotistical that he thought he only had to kiss her and she'd jump back into bed with him? Not when he knew how much she hated him. Or perhaps he looked on her hatred as a challenge, she mused. Something on the lines of if he could get her back he could get anybody. Maybe his appetite for sex was so jaded that he needed that kind of stimulus. Which was a pretty sick thought. Four years ago he hadn't been like that, she thought, remembering. Then they'd revelled in each other's bodies, had delighted to explore and find the ways to give pleasure. She had been almost totally ignorant but Bruno had taught her so much, so many wonderful things.

Her eyes filled with sudden tears and the street became a blur. Norrie dashed them away with an angry hand. That was long over, those months of innocent love, and were best forgotten. She was older now and knew the score. Never again would she let herself fall helplessly in love with someone, never again leave herself open to hurt and humiliation.

It was a couple of days before Dave, her union contact, 'phoned her to say that he'd got the printed leaflets ready to distribute.

'Great,' Norrie enthused. 'When do we start?'

He laughed. 'That's what I like to hear. How about early tomorrow morning as the staff arrive at work?'

'Fine.'

Norrie was outside the *Welford Observer* at seven-thirty the next morning with Ben in his pushchair, warmly wrapped against the early morning chill. Dave strolled along a quarter of an hour later.

'What did you bring him for?' he said disapprovingly, pointing at Ben.

'Because I didn't have anywhere to leave him of course.'

'You can't take a kid on a picket line,' he protested.

'It's hardly a picket line; we're only handing out leaflets. Anyway it will give him the right ideas from an early age,' Norrie said cheerfully. 'Let's have a look at the leaflets.'

Dave took the bundle from an envelope and handed her half. They were printed in red on white paper and looked most impressive with the heading, 'Do you want a say in the future of your paper?' standing out in bold type.

'They look great. Did they print them at headquarters for you?'

Dave laughed. 'You're joking. I did them here yesterday while I was supposed to be printing some posters. I did a load because I thought we could hand them out to passers-by as well. Let them know what's going on.'

'Well, they certainly won't find out from the *Observer*,' Norrie agreed. 'I just hope Bruno Denton doesn't find out that you printed them here,' she added anxiously.

For the next hour they were kept busy handing out leaflets and answering questions from strangers, and the joking, but sometimes scornful, comments of their colleagues. Bruno turned up just after eight and took in the situation at a glance, giving a derisive smile as he took a leaflet from the defiant hand Norrie thrust in front of him. He didn't bother to read it but shoved it in his pocket, his eyes holding hers, before walking on.

For a surprised moment his glance rested on Ben, tucked away in the shelter of the doorway, but just then the editor rushed up and began to tick Norrie and Dave off, and Bruno turned back.

Surprisingly he took their side. 'They are within their rights,' he reminded Harry Simons. 'And they're not trying to stop anyone working. Besides,' he added, 'they're only wasting their time.' And putting a hand under the editor's elbow, he walked with him into the building.

'Phew. What do you make of that?' Dave asked Norrie. 'I thought Harry was going to do his pieces then and stop us distributing any more leaflets.'

'I'm not worried about Harry, after all he's in the union, too, and knew he couldn't really stop us. But I'm surprised that Denton took our side. And I didn't like the way he said we were wasting our time. I'm afraid he might have something up his sleeve,' Norrie answered uneasily.

'He's just trying to scare you,' Dave scoffed. 'Don't take any notice of him. Come on, there's some people getting off that bus.'

They went on handing out the leaflets until all the staff had arrived and then Dave went into work himself, leaving Norrie to give out the last few in the new shopping precinct. By that time Ben had had enough and they were both pleased to go back to the cottage and have a hot drink. She read to him for a while and then left him in his favourite place in front of the television set watching a children's programme while she finished typing out her article on the shell grotto. Norrie had also unearthed quite a lot of information from the county archives and she was quite pleased with her work; at the least it should ensure a lot more visitors for Sid to show round.

At one-fifteen the 'phone rang and Norrie left Ben to eat his lunch alone while she answered. It was Dave. 'You were right,' he said tersely. 'Denton did have something up his sleeve.'

'Why, what's happened?'

'He put a notice up on the board this morning saying that the new mid-week edition would start in three weeks. And he's promised a five per cent pay rise from the first of next month. For everyone, linotypesetters and journalists alike.'

'What about job losses? Did he mention those?'

'No. But the first of the new computers is being installed over this weekend. And they've got some instructors coming down to show the men how to use it, so that it will be all ready for the new print run.'

'Will it put anyone out of work, do you think?'

'Shouldn't think so. Some might have to come in on different days, that's all.'

'How do the men feel about that?'

'They don't seem to mind. Some of them even like the idea. Most of the people here are laughing their heads off at our leaflets now,' he added. 'I tried to tell them that the notice only got put up *after* our leaflets went out, but they mostly seemed to think it was coincidence. Denton's properly spiked our guns,' he said gloomily. 'They should wait until he starts clamping down, that's what I say.'

'Isn't there anything else we can do? Perhaps if you got on to headquarters again?'

'I can try, but I don't think it will do any good. Look, I've got to go, I'm in me lunch hour. See you.'

'Bye.' Norrie put the 'phone down in frustrated anger. Bruno certainly hadn't wasted any time; the staff of the *Observer* would hardly have had time to read and discuss their leaflet before he had announced his juicy titbit, the news of the rise completely covering the fact that the men had arbitrarily got to learn new skills within a matter of weeks as well as doing their normal job. And if they couldn't take to the change, what happened to them then?

Over the next three weeks the newspaper offices were full of the heightened interest and excitement that change brings as some of the old linotype machines were replaced by the new computerised keyboards. Norrie went in on her usual days to collect and hand in her work but everyone was too busy to talk at any length. She got a few jeering remarks from some of the junior journalists and several 'Why don't you wait and see' type comments from their seniors, but there was no one who was really willing to listen or take it further. But then she heard of the first redundancy. Dave told her when she went in one morning.

'But I don't think it's going to make much difference,' he advised. 'It's one of the elderly linotypesetters. They've wrapped it up as early retirement, of course, but he just couldn't get on with the new keyboard computers. I've talked to him and tried to find out whether he was forced to go, but he won't say. Afraid of being thought a fool, I suppose.' He shrugged. 'And I expect the management gave him a retirement payment and told him to keep his mouth shut. It's like hitting your head against a brick wall.'

'Did you try the local union headquarters again?'

'Yes, but they said to wait and see what happens. Said there was nothing yet to warrant them stepping in. Which I've got to admit is true so far.'

'Nevertheless I think I'll write to them myself and send the details about my old paper; that might make them take some notice.'

'It's worth a try, I suppose. But you want to be careful,' he warned. 'You've got that kid to look after and it will hurt you more to get the sack than it will me.'

Norrie smiled at him, appreciating his concern. 'Thanks,' she said warmly. 'But don't worry about me. I'll be okay.'

That afternoon Norrie carefully composed a letter pointing out all the relevant details and asking the union to look into the take-over, bearing in mind Bruno's past record, and sent it off by first class mail. With any luck they should receive it the next day and possibly act on it during the following week.

The weather next day changed completely, bringing one of those cold spells that seem like winter all over again even though it was well into summer. On the Friday afternoon Norrie had to go over to the nearest big town to get some things for Ben that she couldn't buy in Welford. The trip was successful, but towards the end of the afternoon it began to rain quite heavily. Ben was okay under the waterproof cover of his pushchair, but Norrie was loaded up with parcels and had no hand free to carry an umbrella so just had to get wet. To make things worse, the rain had made everyone decide to go home at the same time and the queue for the bus stretched past the shelter so that they had to stand in the open, the rain beating down on them.

The bus was late; it would be of course, and Norrie was beginning to wish she'd never come out. Leaning sideways, she peered past the people in front of her, trying to see if the bus was in sight. A car went by, swishing through the puddles, then it stopped and backed up. She took no notice at first and it wasn't until the electric window on the passenger side slid open and a voice said her name that she realised it was Bruno's car. As she stared in surprise he got out and came round towards her.

'Come on. Get in,' he ordered. 'Give me your shopping.'

'No.' Her instinctive reaction was to refuse and she tried to step away, but there was no room in the tightly packed queue of people. 'I—I don't want a lift.'

'Don't be damn ridiculous,' he said shortly. 'You're soaked.'

'Then I'd make your car wet.'

But he had already opened the boot and firmly took her parcels from her. Then he noticed Ben, who'd been almost hidden by the shopping. 'Is he with you?' he asked in surprise.

'Yes. So I can't come. Please give me my things back.'

Not bothering to argue, Bruno dropped her packages in the boot and said tersely, 'Get in the car with the kid. I'll deal with the pushchair.'

Angry at his arbitrary behaviour, Norrie said, 'I've told you, I don't want a lift. I'd rather wait for the bus.'

'For God's sake, woman, stop arguing and get in the car.'

The people around her were turning to watch and Norrie suddenly felt ridiculous. Unstrapping Ben, she picked him up and got into the back of Bruno's Jaguar, inwardly cursing his high-handedness and hoping that he'd make a fool of himself trying to close the pushchair, which was awkward enough at the best of times. But to her added annoyance Bruno managed it perfectly easily and was back in the car within a couple of minutes. As they drew away she heard a noise behind them and Norrie looked through the rear window to see the bus pull up at the stop. If it had only arrived on time she wouldn't have been put in this unwelcome position.

'You're wet.' Ben pulled himself off her lap on to the seat beside her but Norrie kept a tight hold on the bottom of his anorak; the car had four doors and there were no childproof locks.

'What are you doing with the kid?' Bruno asked over his shoulder.

'I'm—I'm looking after him for someone.' Norrie answered hesitantly, not wanting to talk about anything on a personal level.

'Anyone I know?'

'No. No one you know.'

'You ought to get yourself a car,' Bruno commented. 'Or at least have taken a taxi.'

'They cost too much,' Norrie pointed out tartly. 'And I don't need a car; I can manage perfectly well on public transport.'

Bruno raised a sardonic eyebrow as he glanced back at her, clearly disbelieving. Then his expression changed as he said abruptly, 'Is your job on the *Observer* the only work you do?'

Biting back the impulse to tell him to mind his own business, Norrie answered coldly, 'No, I also do freelance work.'

'Successfully?'

'Successfully enough. Why do you want to know?'

'Just interested, that's all.'

Which could mean anything. But one thing was for sure, he certainly wasn't worrying about what she would live on if he kicked her off the *Observer*.

Ben had been sitting quietly, shy of the big stranger, but now he got more confident and stood up, holding on to the back of the passenger seat. 'What your name?' he demanded.

Norrie tried to shush him, but Bruno gave him an amused glance. 'It's okay. It's Bruno,' he told him.

'Mr Denton,' Norrie corrected dampeningly.

Not a bit discouraged, Ben went on, 'I'm Ben and I'm nearly four.' Adding matter-of-factly, 'Are you my Daddy?'

It was a question he asked all the strange men he came in contact with, but he would have to ask Bruno.

''Fraid not, old son,' he replied cheerfully. Then, to Norrie, 'Doesn't he know who his father is?'

'No. He can't remember him.' And she looked determinedly out of the window, not wanting to talk.

But Ben more than made up for her silence, pointing to the instrument panel and asking, 'What this for? What that do?'

Bruno answered him patiently enough, not talking down to him but merely simplifying his explanations so that Ben could understand.

It seemed to take an age to get to Welford but at last they were in the town and Norrie could say, 'If you'll drop us at the next corner, please.'

'You surely don't live in the centre of the town?'

'No, but we can walk from here.'

'Nonsense, it's still pelting with rain. Tell me where you live.'

Her voice rising, Norrie repeated, 'I said we would walk.'

Bruno stopped at a red light and put an arm across the back of his seat as he turned angrily to face her. 'When are you damn well going to stop arguing with me?'

'When are you leaving Welford?' she countered.

His face grew grim. 'Just as soon as I can.'

'Well, it can't be too soon for me.'

They glared at each other until the car behind hooted and Bruno realised the lights had changed to green. 'Where do you live?' he repeated harshly.

'The next right.'

Beyond directing him, Norrie didn't speak again until Bruno pulled up outside the cottage. It was a small old house with only a tiny garden separating it from the pavement, but the brickwork had mellowed to rose red and Norrie had painted the door white and beside it had planted a climbing rose that was heavy now with yellow blooms, their heads hanging in the rain.

Norrie ran to the door with Ben and quickly unlocked it and shoved him inside while she went back for her things. Bruno was already out of the car and was getting the pushchair out of the boot. 'There was no point in both of us getting wet,' she pointed out acidly, taking the pushchair from him.

Without bothering to answer, Bruno picked up her shopping, banged down the boot lid and followed her up the path to the door. Quickly Norrie dropped the pushchair in the doorway and turned to take the parcels, barring his way. He stood there, bare-headed, the rain trickling down his face like tears and making his thick hair start to curl. 'Aren't you going to ask me in?' he asked with heavy irony.

'No,' Norrie answered coldly. 'I'm not going to let you intrude into my home. Or into my life. Not any more.' Then she stepped inside and shut the door in his face.

CHAPTER FOUR

NORRIE'S letter to the local union headquarters resulted in them sending an official down to Welford a few days later. He arrived quite unannounced and started talking to various members of the staff, working his way through each department of the building before asking to speak to Bruno. Dave had let Norrie know the moment he'd arrived and she hurried to leave Ben with the child-minder and get to the *Observer* as soon as she could, but although she hung around Sue's office all morning, fully expecting the official to want to speak to her, he didn't come near or ask for her.

'Now what do I do?' she asked Sue frustratedly when the office clock showed twelve-thirty. 'I can't hang around here indefinitely.'

'Well, he's got your home 'phone number, hasn't he? If he'd wanted to speak to you he would surely have 'phoned to let you know,' Sue pointed out rather impatiently, getting fed up with having her around. 'Look, if he wants to talk to you, I'll get him to 'phone you from here, okay?'

'Okay. Thanks, Sue. I'm sorry to be a pest,' Norrie sighed. 'I just wish I knew what was happening.'

'Don't we all,' the older woman agreed. 'But I doubt very much whether we'll hear anything today. You know what they're like at headquarters.'

And in fact none of the staff heard anything for several days until everyone received a duplicated letter saying that the union official would address a meeting the following morning. Norrie's copy arrived by post the same day as they were handed out at the office so she had plenty of time to arrange for Ben to be looked after. There was only the notification of the meeting in her letter, nothing different from that of anyone else, not even an acknowledgement of her own letter to the union, which rather annoyed her. They could at least have thanked her for writing to them.

If any major event had happened in the town of Welford or its environs at ten-thirty that Tuesday morning it would have gone unreported, because the entire staff of the *Observer* was gathered in the main office waiting to hear what the two officials from the local union headquarters had to say. Bruno was there, too, plus a man no one had seen before but was rumoured to be Bruno's accountant. Norrie stood towards the back of the room among a group of the other women and made sure she didn't meet Bruno's eyes when he looked round. If he didn't already know that she had written to the union he must surely have guessed.

The union official who'd visited the paper and talked to everyone stood up to speak first. He said that the union had been asked to look into the take-over and that he had gone into it very thoroughly with both staff and management. 'After talking to the new owner,' he went on, 'we are satisfied that there will be no redundancies and that, in fact, more staff will be taken on. There has, however, been some discussion on wage structures and we have now reached agreement on these. These are in addition to the five per cent across the board increase that has already been promised when the new mid-week edition comes out.'

A murmur of pleased surprise ran through the

crowded room at this announcement and increased when he went on to detail the rises. 'So, brothers, as far as the union is concerned,' the man finished, 'the take-over has done nothing but good for the paper. Should the position change in the future, then we will, of course, be ready to step in on your behalf, and we will be keeping a close eye on the development of the paper through your Father of the Chapel. As to the fears of sackings and redundancies that have been expressed, we can only repeat the assurances—that we have also had in writing—from Mr Denton, that the staff levels will be increased and not reduced. Thank you, brothers.' And he sat down amid a spontaneous burst of applause.

As it died down, Bruno got to his feet. 'I should just like to add a few words before the meeting breaks up.' He paused, waiting for complete silence, which he quickly got, then he said clearly, 'It is a mistake to think that the past must be a model for the present. Circumstances are never the same. Times and people change. What was unavoidable in one place is not necessarily so in another. And what happened in the past is over, finished; one should not let it affect one's future actions or feelings.'

He was addressing the whole room and not looking at anyone in particular but Norrie knew quite well that the words were meant for her alone. Quite a few other people in the room knew it, too, which made her cheeks even paler than they might have been. She kept her eyes fixed on the wall above Bruno's head so that her chin was high, but there was no way she could meet anyone's eyes, least of all Bruno's.

'Having said that,' Bruno was continuing, 'I hope that the future relationship between staff and management will be a long and happy one. I certainly intend to do my best to make it so.' He paused for a moment and then his voice became brisk and businesslike, 'During the few weeks I've been here I've been looking into the position and I've discovered that the one paper covers too large an area, without being able to give enough space to some of the new towns that are springing up. So I've decided that we will split the area up into four sections with separate papers for each area. We will open a small office with two or three staff in each section, but the production of the newspapers will be carried out here on the new computerised equipment. I also intend to bring in new photographic reproduction equipment and . . .'

His voice went on but Norrie wasn't listening any more. She didn't have to look at the pleased faces around her to know that Bruno had won—and had made her look stupid in the process. For the second time he had ground her face into the dirt. Pure hatred ran through her and she longed to hit back, to hurt him as he'd hurt her, but all she could do was to stand there and wait, to listen as everyone burst into loud and prolonged applause as he finished speaking. Wait while the Editor thanked him on behalf of the staff for everything he was doing for them. Wait while the union official complimented him on the way he'd accepted their proposals. Wait, and go on waiting until she wanted to scream out her hatred, to scream and scream at the top of her voice.

'Come back to my office with me.' Sue's touch on her arm brought Norrie back to reality. It was over at last and Bruno had left the room with the Editor and union officials. People were going back to their offices, were giving her odd looks as they passed. She nodded and followed the other woman, not speaking until they reached Sue's office.

'Here, you look as if you could do with a drink.' Sue poured out a couple of whiskies and put one into her hand.

'Thanks,' Norrie drank it down in one gulp and then sighed. 'So he's won,' she said bitterly. 'No one will listen to me now.'

'Maybe he has changed,' Sue suggested. 'Perhaps he was right to act the way he did on your old paper.'

'Et tu, Brute,' Norrie said with bitter sarcasm, putting down her glass.

'That was hardly fair. Bruno hasn't behaved anything like the way you described since he's been here,' the older woman pointed out.

'No, I'm sorry.' She stood up. 'Who do I hand my resignation to, you or the editor?'

Sue looked at her in consternation. 'But you don't have to leave. Bruno said there wouldn't be any redundancies.'

'You don't really think I'm going to stay on and work for him, do you? Surely you can see it's impossible?'

'But what will you do? You might not be able to get a job on another paper.'

'It doesn't matter. There must be some work I can do, even if it's only scrubbing floors.'

'Don't be stupid,' Sue's voice rose angrily. 'You can't just walk out of this job. What about Ben? You've got to think of him. You must remember that as a one-parent family you've got responsibilities that you can't just . . .'

She stopped abruptly. Norrie followed her eyes and saw Bruno standing in the doorway. She hadn't heard the door open so it must have been ajar. There was a peculiar look on his face, as if he was drunk or had been punched on the jaw.

Norrie swung angrily round to face him. 'Well, I
suppose you'll do just as well,' she said bitterly. 'In
fact it will probably make your day even more
successful. You've got what you want. I'm leaving.
Now.' And she strode towards the door.

For a moment he didn't react but then moved to
stop her. 'Wait. I want to talk to you.'

But he was too late, Norrie brushed past him and
walked out of the room and down the corridor. As she
went she heard Sue say to him, 'Why don't you talk to
me instead?'

And she'd thought Sue was her friend! Well, she
certainly hadn't wasted any time in changing sides,
Norrie thought savagely, but then was instantly filled
with depression. What right had she to criticise Sue?
After all, the other girl's whole livelihood depended on
how well she got on with Bruno. And it had been
pretty obvious from the start that Sue fancied him.
Well, she was welcome to him.

Norrie had no belongings to collect, no desk to
clear, all she had to do was to step out of the door into
the street and that would be it, she would be without a
job. But she took the step all the same, walking
determinedly out of the building and quickly away
without once looking back.

The sensible thing would be to pick up Ben from
the child-minder straight away and save some money,
but Norrie was feeling far from sensible today and just
wanted to be alone for a while, so she walked to the
park and sat on a wooden bench beneath the broken
walls of an ancient castle overgrown with a riot of
climbing plants. It was peaceful here, she could close
her eyes and listen to the birds singing in the trees,
feel the sun on her face and smell the newly-cut grass.
Pleasant sensations that would go on, no matter what.

It helped to give her a sense of perspective about the future but it didn't allay her present feelings of outraged bitterness and depression. At the moment she felt as if everything Bruno had done for the *Observer* had been to spite her. Would he have been so generous if she hadn't been there to reveal the truth about his past? She couldn't see it. And in a year or so inflation would catch up with the rises he had given them, but would the staff then get another increase? Enough to cover the extra work they would have to do to publish five newspapers instead of one? Norrie greatly doubted it. And in the meantime she was out of a job. Tears came to Norrie's eyes and she let them fall. There was no one to see, not even Ben. For once she could give way to her emotions.

Her eyes were still red nearly an hour later when Norrie went to collect Ben, but she covered them with a pair of sunglasses and the child-minder didn't notice. Her fee took nearly all the cash Norrie had but she just didn't feel up to going back into the town to the bank. Taking hold of Ben's hand she began to walk him home, but he was feeling active and wanted to play all the time, climbing on to walls and trying to play hide and seek with her. Usually Norrie would have joined in but today she just wasn't in the mood. As they neared the cottage he started to run through an alleyway into a nearby field where he often picked wild flowers.

'Ben. Not today. Come on,' she called to him. And then, when he took no notice, 'Ben, come here this minute. Do you want me to smack you?'

He came at that, looking up at her with such puzzled eyes that Norrie immediately felt a louse. Tentatively he stretched out his little fat hand full of buttercups, offering them to her. Silly tears pricked her eyes again and she knelt to hug him. 'Oh Ben, I'm sorry. I didn't mean to shout.' She put her face against his soft skin and held him tightly for a moment until he wriggled free.

'Look, Norrie. Man,' he said in her ear.

Opening her eyes, Norrie blinked away the tears and saw a tall, dark shape looming over them. Then her eyes widened as she saw that it was Bruno. Quickly she got to her feet and instinctively took hold of Ben's hand, pulling him behind her. 'What do you want?' she demanded, using her fingers to dry her eyes.

He didn't answer for several minutes, he was staring down at Ben and there was such a grim look on his face that Norrie was frightened. Scooping the boy up into her arms, she went to walk past him, but Bruno shot out his hand and caught her wrist. 'I want to talk to you,' he said for the second time that day, but this time there was far more menace in his tone.

'But I don't want to talk to you, not now or ever.' She began to move towards the cottage but Bruno came along with her, so she stood still again. 'Will you please go away? I've told you, I have nothing to say to you.'

'But I'm quite sure that you do,' Bruno told her forcefully, and began to pull her up the path to the cottage.

'Let go of me.' Norrie tried to pull free but was hampered by carrying Ben and her handbag. 'If you don't let go of me I'll scream,' she threatened.

'Okay, go ahead and scream.' Bruno let go of her suddenly but instead grabbed Ben out of her arms.

Norrie's face went deathly pale and she tried to snatch the child back. 'Give him to me. How *dare* you touch him?'

But Bruno kept a tight hold on the boy. 'I'll give him back to you as soon as we get inside.'

She stared at him, seeing the uncompromising determination in his face, and then looked at the fright in Ben's eyes as he was held in the stranger's arms. And, seeing that, Norrie knew that she had no choice. Quickly she fumbled in her bag for her key and unlocked the door. Bruno followed her inside and shouldered the door shut behind him.

'Give him to me.' Norrie's voice rose hysterically.

Bruno's eyes went round the little sitting-room, taking in the toys, the childish drawings pinned to the wall, the kangaroo height chart on the back of the door, and his face became even grimmer. But he gave Ben back to her.

Norrie hugged the child close for a moment, then put him down and helped him off with his anorak. 'Go and put your coat away, poppet,' she told him as calmly as she could, hating that frightened look in his eyes. 'And then you'd better find a lettuce leaf for Henry. I expect he's hungry.' Henry was the guinea-pig.

'I'm hungry, too,' Ben pointed out, holding on to her hand and looking up at Bruno uneasily.

'I'll get you something soon. Go on. It's all right.' She gave him a little push and he went into the kitchen. Then Norrie straightened and faced Bruno. 'Just what the hell do you want? How dare you force your way in here.'

Anger flared in Bruno's dark eyes. 'I want the truth. All of it.'

Norrie glared back at him. 'Very well, you can have it. Although I'm sure you must have guessed by now.'

His eyes widened as he stared at her, but then he

said in a soft, almost stunned voice, 'But I want to hear it from you.'

She shrugged, puzzled by his tone. 'All right. I was the one who wrote to the union and told them of the way you used the staff on the Devon paper—or rather the way you mis-used them. So you needn't try pinning the blame on anyone else; I acted entirely on my own initiative. And I'm glad I did. At least it has stopped you from sacking anyone here.'

Her voice tailed off as Bruno shook his head at her. 'I didn't come here because of that. I couldn't care less what you told the union about me. I'll make exactly what changes I want whether they like it or not.'

'Then why did you come here?'

He hesitated a moment, his eyes searching her face, but turned as Ben came into the room. 'I came here,' he said slowly, 'because of him.'

Norrie's first reaction, before she even began to think, was one of protectiveness. 'He's nothing to do with you,' she said sharply and caught hold of Ben's hand, pulling him towards her.

'Isn't he? That's what I came to find out.'

Norrie stared at him, not understanding, thinking only that he represented some threat to Ben. Perhaps was going to try and get him taken away from her because she no longer had a job, say she wasn't fit to look after him or something. He was looking at her so strangely. 'You keep away from him. I told you; I'm looking after him for someone,' she told him wildly.

'But I don't believe you. I think he's yours,' Bruno said grimly, his eyes again on her face.

'That isn't true. He's not mine.' For the life of her she couldn't see where this was leading, but Bruno looked so menacing that she was frightened.

'You liar!' he shot at her. 'Look at him; his hair, his

eyes; he's the exact duplicate of you.' Squatting down to Ben's height, he smiled at the boy and said gently, 'Hallo, old son. You haven't told me your name yet.'

Norrie moved to interrupt, but Bruno glanced up at her and said sharply, 'Let him speak for himself. What is your name?' he asked Ben again.

His little hand tightened on Norrie's as Ben glanced up at her uncertainly, but then he looked at Bruno. 'Ben Peters,' he said clearly.

'And how old are you? Do you know?'

''Course I know. I'm nearly four. And I can read lots of words. And I know all the A, B, C. And I can count up to a hundred—two hundred,' he amended. Not one to keep his talents hidden was Ben.

'Bet you don't know when your birthday is, though,' Bruno prodded.

'Yes, I do. It's the twenty-seventh of September.'

And suddenly Norrie knew why Bruno was asking all these questions, why he had forced his way into the house, and why he had that terribly grim look on his face. The colour drained out of her own cheeks and when Ben looked up at her and said, 'That's right, isn't it? The twenty-seventh of September?' she could only nod and say faintly, 'Yes, that's right, poppet.'

Slowly Bruno straightened, his angry eyes staring into hers. 'So now we both know the truth,' he said bleakly. 'So now let's talk.'

'Darling, why don't you go upstairs and look at your storybooks for a while?' Norrie suggested to Ben. His ears were already pricking up and she didn't want to have to discuss his father in front of him.

'But I'm hungry,' he wailed.

'I'll find you a biscuit.' She took him into the kitchen and took a packet of biscuits from its hiding place, thinking that the mistake Bruno had made about

Ben would be laughable if she didn't hate him so much. But at least she could let him know in very derisory terms that the mistake was a stupid one. As if Ben could possibly be his child! Ben was far too nice.

Ben went happily off upstairs with his plate of biscuits and Norrie returned to the sitting-room. Bruno was looking at one of Ben's drawings on the wall. It showed three people with the names Ben, Norrie, Daddy written underneath them; Ben was obviously himself and he had taken pains to fill in Norrie's long hair and her flowered dress, but the third figure was a complete blank. Ben had no ideas on daddies at all. When Bruno turned round, Norrie had the biggest shock of her life; his eyes were wet with tears. 'Why the hell didn't you tell me?' he demanded savagely. 'Didn't it occur to you that I had a right to know my own child?'

Norrie was so taken aback that she could only stare at him in stunned astonishment, quite incapable of answering.

Striding over to her, Bruno took hold of her shoulders, his grip hurting. 'Didn't what we had together mean anything to you at all?' When she didn't speak his eyes grew bleak. 'My God, did you hate me so much that you wouldn't even tell me?' His fingers tightened angrily for a moment, but then he pushed her away from him as if he found her repulsive and strode to the window, standing with his back to her, his hands gripping the sill. 'Were you afraid that I wouldn't stand by you? Was that it?'

Norrie was still gazing at him in amazement, taking in his scarcely controlled fury, the whiteness of his knuckles, and the bleakness in his eyes. He cared! He really cared! *My God, it would serve him damn well right if Ben was his!* But she said again, in an unsteady voice, 'Ben is nothing to do with you.'

Bruno swung round. 'You liar! Everything fits. We were together all that winter four years ago.' His mouth thinned into a sneer. 'Unless, of course, you were having an affair with someone else at the same time.'

Norrie's cheeks flamed. 'You know damn well that I wasn't. I made such a fool of myself over you that I didn't even look at another man.'

'So that proves it then, doesn't it?' Bruno moved across to stand in front of her, his dark eyes fixed intently on her face. 'He's mine, isn't he? Admit it.'

As she gazed defiantly up at him, the wish to hurt came flooding back. And if the only way she could hurt him was through Ben . . . Did she dare let him go on thinking that Ben was his child? Norrie lowered her head to avoid his searching eyes. But no, she couldn't do it. Although it would have been a sweet revenge for what Bruno had done to her, and to her father. Especially for his sake. Without looking at him she said, 'No. No, he isn't.'

Putting his hand under her chin, Bruno forced her head up so that she had to look at him. 'Now say that again,' he demanded cruelly.

She tried to push his hand away. 'You're hurting me.'

'Don't try and evade the issue. I want the truth.'

Norrie's temper suddenly flared and she put her hands against his chest and pushed him away with all her strength. 'Who the hell do you think you are? And what makes you think you can force your way in here and start throwing your weight about? Now get out. D'you hear me? Get out or I'll 'phone the police and have you thrown out.'

'Nice try,' Bruno told her bitingly. 'But you needn't think you can fob me off so easily. Why else would an unmarried girl be looking after a child unless he was her own? And he's so like you that he couldn't be anyone else's.' Lifting a hand, he traced his finger along the line of her jaw and down her throat while Norrie stared at him balefully.

'He could belong to a member of my family,' she pointed out. 'My brother, for example.'

He laughed. 'I seem to remember that your brother is happily married and probably has a family of his own by now.' His finger grew still. 'Why did you go through with having Ben? You could have had an abortion. Or had him adopted, even. But you chose to keep him and bring him up on your own, even though you must have realised the difficulties it involved. So why?'

Norrie moved away from him. 'Mind your own damn business.'

Catching her arm, Bruno angrily pulled her back. 'It is my business. And I am involved, whether you like it or not. Now that I've found out about Ben there's no way I'm just going to walk away and forget about him. He's as much mine as yours and I'm . . .'

'No, he isn't,' Norrie told him forcefully. 'I've told you, he's nothing . . .'

'Don't try and shut me out,' Bruno interjected. 'You may have had him to yourself up to now, but from now on you're going to have to learn to share him.'

Norrie laughed scathingly. 'And how do you intend to do that—by sending him birthday and Christmas presents every year from whatever part of the country you happen to be in?'

His voice cold, Bruno answered, 'Oh, but I'm going

to take a much closer interest in him than that. I'm going to marry you and legally adopt him.'

For the second time that afternoon Norrie could only stare at him speechlessly, but then she began to laugh, little giggles that grew inside her until she was doubled up with laughter, tears streaming down her face. 'You want to—you want to marry me. Oh God, that's funny. That's really funny.'

'Shut up. You're getting hysterical. If you don't stop it I shall have to slap you,' he warned when she sank into a chair, still convulsed with laughter. 'What's so damn funny about it anyway?'

'You are,' Norrie told him, sobering suddenly. 'What you're suggesting is utterly ridiculous.'

'He's my kid and I want to share him,' Bruno repeated obstinately, his jaw thrusting forward.

'But haven't you forgotten one small point?' she asked with heavy sarcasm. 'You're the last man on earth I'd ever want to marry.'

'But you're going to all the same. I'm not going to let any kid of mine be brought up in these conditions.'

Norrie stood up and faced him. 'And just what's wrong with this house?' she demanded truculently.

For a moment Bruno's eyes softened as he said, 'Nothing. I'm sure you've done your best. But,' he gave a helpless kind of shrug. 'Look, I'm not trying to offend you in any way or belittle what you've done, but I'm in a pretty good position financially now and I can give him so much more. Both of you so much more.'

'I'm not exactly a pauper, you know,' Norrie informed him, her cheeks flushed. 'I own this cottage and I still have some money that my father left me.'

'But how long will that last now that you've left the *Welford Observer*?' He raised a hand to stop her when she was about to speak. 'Okay, I know that you can probably get another job, but it will mean having Ben looked after by strangers, and I don't want that.'

'Don't you indeed?' Norrie glared at him and suddenly realised she was arguing with him as if Ben really was his child. It brought her up short and she realised that she must end this before it went any further. But he seemed so sure, so convinced that Ben was his. Bruno was making a bigger fool of himself with every word he said, and Norrie rather enjoyed making a fool of him. So, perversely, she decided to play him along a little longer.

'No, I don't. Small children like Ben should have their mothers to look after them. And what about his education; can you afford to pay for that?'

'By that I suppose you mean can I afford to send him to a private school. No, I can't, but an ordinary state school was good enough for me and it will be good enough for Ben.'

'But it isn't good enough for my son,' Bruno informed her tersely, his face determined.

Norrie stared at him, then, unable to resist, said, 'What makes you so absolutely certain that Ben is your child? I haven't said that he is.'

'You didn't have to. I was told quite definitely that he was mine.'

'You were told?' Norrie's eyes widened in astonishment. 'Who by?'

'By Sue Stewart. After you walked out of her office this morning, having made your grand gesture, she said that she knew about our affair and then asked me why I wasn't man enough to face up to the responsibilities of my own child. Which was quite a staggering question to have thrown at me,' he added sardonically.

Norrie was pretty staggered herself. She had no idea that Sue had put that interpretation on what she'd told her. 'She should never have done that,' Norrie murmured, half to herself. 'She had no right to say anything to you.'

'No, she didn't,' Bruno agreed coldly. '*You* were the one who should have told me, right from the start.'

'It wouldn't have made any difference,' Norrie pointed out, unable to resist carrying on with the act. 'I wouldn't have married you any more then than I would now. I hated you for what you did to my father, and my feelings haven't changed in the last four years.'

'Four years ago you said that you loved me,' Bruno pointed out, his eyes fixed on her face. 'Among other things you also said I meant more to you than anything else in the world and that you would . . .'

'Shut up! I was infatuated by you then, that was all. You can be very charming when you want to. When you want to use someone. And I was stupid enough to fall for it. But my feelings soon changed when I found out what you were really like. I thought I made that quite clear at the time,' she added derisively.

Bruno sat down in her favourite armchair, his long legs stretched out casually in front of him. 'At the time you were upset and not thinking clearly. Added to which, your father was doing his best to come between us. He hated the thought of having a son-in-law who knew him to be inefficient and unbusinesslike.'

'That's a lie. He was perfectly capable of running that paper.'

'Rubbish. It had been going downhill almost from the moment he took it over. It was one of the most antiquated local papers in the country. And he knew it but couldn't face up to the fact and let someone else take over.'

Her eyes flashing angrily, Norrie said, 'We're never going to agree on that or anything else, so why don't you just get out of here?'

'We haven't settled when we're going to get married yet,' Bruno reminded her calmly.

Norrie gasped. 'I wouldn't marry you if you were the last man on earth.'

He laughed, and it was as if she were hearing an old song that she had loved and hadn't heard for a long time, it brought back so many memories of youth and happiness. 'Somehow I don't think you'd stand a chance. Unless I rescued you from getting killed in the rush.'

She wanted to smile, but stopped herself because she knew it would be a small victory for him. 'I shall never marry you, not under any circumstances, and that's final. So will you please go. Ben's hungry and so am I.'

'So let me take you both out to lunch.'

'No.' She looked at him antagonistically. 'We don't need you or your money. So just leave us alone.'

Bruno stood up. 'I don't give up that easily. You should know that I'm not afraid to take up a challenge.'

'It wasn't a challenge. It was a statement. We don't want you.'

For a moment his eyes flamed with anger but he quickly controlled it. 'I'm not going to let you shut me out from my own child—even if I have to take legal steps to gain access to him.'

'You wouldn't dare!'

'Oh, yes I would. I'll fight you for him if I have to.' He paused to add emphasis, then said, 'And I always win any fight I undertake. You should know that. So you might just as well accept the inevitable and marry me. You will in the end, anyway.'

Norrie smiled coldly. 'That's where you're wrong. This is one fight that you don't stand a chance of winning. Because you'll never be able to prove that Ben is yours.'

'Is he mine?'

'No.'

Bruno grinned. 'You're getting quite good at lying. I could almost have believed you then. But you've left it too late to try and convince me now. Ben's mine and you're not going to keep him from me.' He raised a hand in mock salute. 'Goodbye—for now.'

He left, closing the door behind him, and the room seemed suddenly much larger and very empty. Norrie's knees felt weak and she sank into the nearest chair, which happened to be the one that Bruno had just vacated, and when she felt its warmth she hastily got up again. Her mind was in a whirl, filled with a crazy kind of excitement that Bruno had made such a silly mistake and she'd let him go on thinking it. She laughed aloud as she remembered the way he had completely disbelieved her, even when she'd come right out and told him that Ben wasn't his. Deceiving him gave her a feeling of power over him that she had never felt before. And it felt good. She had been able to hurt him because of his feelings of possessiveness towards what he thought was his son. And she had enjoyed seeing him hurt. It was a very minor repayment for the hurt he had done to her. She could almost wish that Ben really was his son so that she could go on turning the screw, perhaps indefinitely. For a few minutes she let her mind roam free, thinking of a future in which she would have Bruno at her mercy and of all the things she could do to make his life as miserable as he had made hers.

The old grandfather clock that Norrie had brought with her from her father's house chimed the hour and broke into her thoughts. Ben! She'd completely forgotten him. Hastily she ran upstairs to his room, wondering why he was so quiet and afraid that he was either up to mischief or something had happened to him. It wasn't like him to be quiet for more than ten minutes at a time. But he was asleep, curled up on his bed with his fair hair falling over his face. Poor darling, he must have got fed up waiting for his lunch. Leaning over him, Norrie gently brushed the lock of hair off his forehead. How innocent he looked when he was asleep, so angelic that you'd never believe the mischief he could get up to when he was awake. A fiercely protective feeling filled her heart. How *dare* Bruno just walk in here and demand to take Ben over? What did he think the child was—just another newspaper? she thought indignantly.

Ben stirred so she moved away and sat on one of the big cushions on the floor. The room was small with a sloping ceiling and rather dark because there was only a dormer window to light it, but Norrie had done her best to cheer it up, painting the woodwork a warm honey colour and papering the walls with Ben's favourite Mr Men wallpaper. She looked round, resenting Bruno's implication that she couldn't provide for Ben, but then remembered that he had admitted that she was doing all she could for him. Norrie frowned, thinking how different Bruno seemed. His character in some ways seemed far more complex than four years ago. But four years ago she had been in love with him and he could do no wrong in her eyes until his shattering betrayal. And, let's face it, it had been such a highly sexual affair that she had been unable to think of anything else, had been blind to what was going on around her. They had made love as often as they could, mostly at the flat that Bruno had rented in the town, sometimes spending the whole day in bed, but always meeting as often as they possibly could. For a few months she had felt that life was absolutely perfect and she had lived for nothing but to be near Bruno, the hours dragging until they could be together. She longed for his touch, to hear his voice, just to look at him, even. And when she did see him her whole being throbbed with excitement and anticipation so that sometimes it was difficult to breathe. When he touched her her heart did crazy somersaults and she wanted desperately to go to bed with him. Wanted to lie beneath him and have his hard body thrust her into the giddy heights of ecstasy. And he knew it, too. His dark eyes would fill with triumphant amusement when he saw the desire in her face and he would occasionally tease her by holding her close against him when they were in a public place, at a dance or walking along the street, and it would drive her mad with frustration. But it worked both ways because it drove Bruno crazy, too, and then they would abruptly leave or go back to his car and Bruno would drive fast to his flat and hurry inside. And by then their need would be so urgent that there wouldn't even be time to take off all their clothes before he pulled her down on to the floor or the bed and made love to her.

Norrie's hands trembled as she remembered and she had to wipe away a silly tear. All she had wanted out of life, then, was to marry Bruno. To be near him for the rest of her days—and nights. To make love and to have his children. Children that might have looked like Ben, she supposed, or like Bruno. Once she had often pictured the children they would have together, and perhaps, after she'd told him she never wanted to see him again, she had been as miserable about the things that never now would be as much as for the things she'd had and lost. Norrie laughed silently. That Bruno should ask her to marry him now was the height of irony. And especially because he'd been completely misinformed. It would serve him right if she did agree to marry him and turned his life into a hell on earth. Just like hers had been hell for such a long time—and still was in many ways, in the long, lonely nights when her body craved for his touch, his love.

Once, to her shame, she had almost gone to bed with another man to exorcise the memory of Bruno out of her heart and her mind. But it hadn't worked, it had been the most terrible night of her life. Because she couldn't give herself without love, her body had shrunk from physical commitment and she had been wooden and frigid. She had quite liked the man before, but afterwards, when it was thankfully all over, they both knew that they would never see each other again. That had been over two years ago now, but Norrie had never met another man that she had even contemplated having a close relationship with. Once bitten twice shy. Although of course at the back of her mind there was always the hope that one day the right man would come along.

Sighing, Norrie stood up and looked down at Ben again; it was time to wake him or he wouldn't sleep tonight. How sweet, she thought, how very, very sweet a repayment it would be if she married Bruno and then told him that Ben wasn't his son, that he'd been incredibly foolish enough to marry her just to give a name to a child that wasn't even his. Impossible, of course, but what a wonderfully apt revenge.

CHAPTER FIVE

The first intimation that Bruno hadn't given up arrived outside the house at around eleven-thirty the next morning in the shape of a brand new car. It was a small hatchback, ideal for loading Ben's pushchair and, as the salesman who delivered it assured her, easy to drive and economical to run. 'And it's all taxed and insured of course,' he pointed out. 'Mr Denton took care of all that when he came in and bought it this morning. So you'll be able to drive it straight away.' He held out the keys but when Norrie didn't move, added, 'Would you like me to take you out for a ride in it first so that you can get used to the controls?'

Walking forward, Norrie opened the door of the car and looked inside. The front seats still had their thin plastic covers over them and it smelt new and clean, a stimulating smell that made her want to get inside and drive it. But instead she shut the door and walked round the car, the sun reflecting off its shiny blue paintwork and polished chrome. It was exactly the sort of car she would have picked herself, if she'd had a choice, just right for her and Ben. But she hadn't been given a choice. Turning to the salesman she said shortly, 'Take it back.'

His eyebrows rose at least an inch. 'But why? Don't you like it?' he spluttered. 'I might be able to get a different colour for you.'

'Oh, there's nothing wrong with the car. I just don't want it.'

'But it's all paid for. It isn't going to cost you

anything,' he hastened to assure her. 'It's a present from Mr Denton.'

'But maybe I don't want to accept presents from Mr Denton,' Norrie pointed out. 'I'm sorry, but you'll have to take it back.'

He started to argue but gave up when Norrie shook her head determinedly. 'You're mad,' he exclaimed. 'Nobody turns down a free car.'

Norrie laughed as she turned to go into the house. 'Well, I do. There's no way I'm going to accept it, so please don't try bringing it here again.'

She went back to an article she was writing which she hoped would be accepted by the local county magazine, but was interrupted an hour later by an imperative knock on the front door. Glancing out of the window, Norrie saw the blue car again parked outside and gave a snort of annoyance. Why hadn't the silly man listened to her? Opening the door fiercely, she cried, 'Now look here, I told you that I didn't . . .' Her angry words trailed off as she saw not the salesman but Bruno standing on the doorstep. And he was frowning.

'That you didn't want the car,' he finished for her, and pushed his way into the house.

'No, I don't. You're the last person I'd accept presents from, especially something as expensive as a car.'

'It wasn't only for you, it was for Ben as well. He could have caught a chill in that bus queue in the pouring rain.'

'Nonsense, he was perfectly dry in his pushchair. I was the one who was getting wet.'

'All the more reason, then, to take the car,' Bruno pointed out brusquely.

Norrie glared at him impatiently. 'Look, there's no point in arguing; I'm not going to accept it, so you can

YOUR
DREAMS
CAN
COME
TRUE

H·A·R·L·E·Q·U·I·N
FIRST·CLASS
Sweepstakes

Enter and you can win a
◆ ROLLS-ROYCE™   ◆ TRIP TO PARIS   ◆ MINK COAT

A FIRST CLASS OPPORTUNITY FOR YOU

♦ **Grand Prize** – Rolls-Royce ™
  (or $100,000)
♦ **Second Prize** – A trip for two to Paris
  via The Concorde
♦ **Third Prize** – A Luxurious Mink Coat

The Romance can last forever... when you take advantage of this no cost special introductory offer.

4 "HARLEQUIN PRESENTS®" – FREE!   Take four of the world's greatest love stories – FREE from Harlequin Reader Service®! Each of these novels is your free passport to bright new worlds of love, passion and foreign adventure!

But wait...there's _even more_ to this great _free offer_...

HARLEQUIN TOTE BAG – FREE!   Carry away your favourite romances in your elegant canvas Tote Bag. With a snap-top and double handles, your Tote Bag is valued at $6.99 – _but it's yours free with this offer!_

SPECIAL EXTRAS – FREE!   You'll get our free monthly newsletter, packed with news on your favourite writers, upcoming books, and more. Four times a year, you'll receive our members' magazine, Harlequin Romance Digest®!

MONEY-SAVING HOME DELIVERY!   Join Harlequin Reader Service® and enjoy the convenience of previewing eight new books every month, delivered right to your home. _Great savings_ plus _total convenience_ add up to a sweetheart of a deal for you.

BONUS MYSTERY GIFT!   P.S. For a limited time only you will be eligible to receive a _mystery gift free_!

TO EXPERIENCE A WORLD OF ROMANCE.

How to Enter Sweepstakes & How to get 4 FREE BOOKS, A FREE TOTE BAG and A BONUS MYSTERY GIFT.

1. Check ONLY ONE OPTION BELOW.
2. Detach Official Entry Form and affix proper postage.
3. Mail Sweepstakes Entry Form before the deadline date in the rules.

H·A·R·L·E·Q·U·I·N
FIRST·CLASS
Sweepstakes

OFFICIAL ENTRY FORM

Check one:

☐ Yes. Enter me in the Harlequin First Class Sweepstakes and send me 4 FREE HARLEQUIN PRESENTS® novels plus a FREE Tote Bag and a BONUS Mystery Gift. Then send me 8 brand new HARLEQUIN PRESENTS® novels every month as they come off the presses. Bill me at the low price of $1.75 each (a savings of $0.20 off the retail price). There are no shipping, handling or other hidden charges. I understand that the 4 Free Books, Tote Bag and Mystery Gift are mine to keep with <u>no obligation to buy</u>.

☐ No. I don't want to receive the Four Free HARLEQUIN PRESENTS® novels, a Free Tote Bag and a Bonus Gift. However, I <u>do</u> wish to enter the sweepstakes. Please notify me if I win.

See back of book for official rules and regulations.
Detach, affix postage and mail Official Entry Form today!

108–CIP–CAJ4

FIRST NAME_____ LAST NAME_____
                                    (Please Print)
ADDRESS_____ APT._____

CITY_____

PROV./STATE_____ POSTAL CODE/ZIP_____
"Subscription Offer limited to one per-household and not valid to current Harlequin Presents® subscribers. Prices subject to change."

ENTER THE H·A·R·L·E·Q·U·I·N
FIRST·CLASS *Sweepstakes*

Detach, Affix Postage and Mail Today!

Harlequin First Class Sweepstakes
P.O. Box 52010
Phoenix, AZ 85072-9987

just return it to the garage and get your money back. If they'll give it to you.'

'You weren't always so reluctant to take presents from me,' Bruno reminded her.

'That was—different.' Norrie looked away, remembering the things he'd given her during their brief months together: the gold chain bracelet for Christmas, an unusual stone they'd found on the beach, a china figurine, a plastic ring from a bonbon they'd pulled together and Bruno had teasingly put on her engagement finger. She had them still, although she'd been going to throw them away a dozen times, but somehow when it came to it she had been unable to bear parting with them.

'Do you still have them?' Bruno asked, his head tilted so that he could see her face.

Norrie laughed derisively. 'You flatter yourself. Do you really think that I'd want to keep anything that reminded me of you?'

Bruno's jaw hardened, but he said, 'Why not? We had some good times together.'

'Did we? I don't remember.'

'Liar. You remember as well as I do.'

'Then let's just say that I prefer to forget. All I remember about you is the way you kicked my father off his own paper.'

'It was hardly that. And if you would face facts instead of judging it on an emotional level, you'd realise that I had no alternative . . .'

Norrie suddenly turned on him furiously. 'What the hell other level is there? I was in love with you, and yet you did something that hurt my father so much that he didn't want to live any more. Do you think that car crash he died in was an accident? Well, I don't. I know that he wanted to die.'

'And you're blaming me for his death, is that it?' Bruno's jaw thrust forward. 'There's no way you're going to make me feel guilty because of that. Your father was a grown man. What happened to him has happened to nearly three million others, and he should have had the courage to face it like everybody else.'

'Are you saying that he was weak?' Norrie bristled.

'I'm not saying that he was anything. I'm not going to let you try to push the responsibility for his death on to me, that's all.'

Norrie gripped the back of a chair and said tensely, 'He was *my father*. If you had really loved me as you said you did you would have let him stay on as the editor until he retired.'

'And let the paper go on going downhill for another ten years? I bent over backwards to give him time to face reality and see that he had to change with the times, but he was as stubborn as a mule. And you're just as bad,' he added roundly. 'Once you get an idea fixed in your head you won't even consider that you could be wrong.'

'If by that you mean that I should believe your version of what happened, then the answer's no,' Norrie retorted doggedly.

Bruno made an impatient sound and half turned away, but then sighed and said, 'Look, nothing we say or do is going to change the past. It happened and it's over. What we have to think about now is the future, and most specifically Ben's future.'

'That's none of your business.'

Anger flashed in Bruno's eyes as he said exasperatedly, 'We've already gone into that and I don't intend to start arguing all over again. If you won't accept the car as a present, then you can look on it as a company car to go with your job.'

Norrie smiled rather grimly and said with mock sweetness, 'How very kind of you. Only you seem to have forgotten that I don't work for you any longer. I resigned yesterday.'

'But I didn't accept it.'

'You don't have any choice. You can't force me to work for you.'

'You seem to forget that you signed a contract in which two months' notice of termination of employment had to be given by either side.'

Norrie gave a disbelieving laugh. 'You're not going to hold me to that, surely? Not in the circumstances?'

'What circumstances exactly?'

'Well, the fact that I can't stand the new managing director plays a large part in it,' she informed him acidly.

'Does it indeed? Well, that's a pity because you're just going to have to get used to having me around when we're married.'

'You're not still on about that? You can't be serious.'

'I was never more serious about anything in my life. And I've already made enquiries at the local Registrar's Office. We can be married in three weeks' time.'

Norrie gasped. 'You're crazy. You know I'd never marry you.'

'Oh, but you will. I shall need your birth certificate for the marriage licence, by the way.'

'I won't give it to you,' she said defiantly.

But Bruno was quite unperturbed. 'Okay, then I'll get a copy of it.'

'You can't do that. I won't let you.'

'You can't stop me. Anyone can get a copy of the birth certificate of anyone they like.'

It was probably true; Norrie didn't know, but she wondered if, at the same time, he would check on Ben's birth details. He would get a nasty shock if he did, she thought with inward malice. 'You'd be wasting your time. The whole idea is—is preposterous. What's the point of getting married, even for Ben's sake, when we both hate each other?'

Bruno raised a quizzical eyebrow. 'I don't ever recall saying that I hated you.'

Norrie's eyes flew to meet his and were held by their intensity. Her heart gave a crazy lurch and her throat suddenly felt dry so that she had to swallow before she could speak. 'That—that has nothing to do with it.'

'Doesn't it? I should have thought it had everything to do with it.' He moved closer to her and put a hand on her shoulder.

'Don't touch me.' She moved quickly away.

'You liked me to touch you once,' he reminded her.

'But I don't now. And you're the one who said that the past is best forgotten. You can't have it both ways.'

'No, you're right,' he admitted. 'But there are some things that you just can't forget.'

'That's exactly what I feel about my father,' Norrie exclaimed triumphantly.

But Bruno didn't seem to hear as he went on softly, 'Like the way you looked when you opened your eyes after I'd made love to you; like a child who had been given such a wonderful present that she can't believe it's true. And the way you snuggled up to me in your sleep. And then of course there was the way you . . .'

'*Shut up!* I don't want to hear it.' Her cheeks flaming, Norrie strode over to the door and jerked it open. 'Get out of here.'

'What's the matter? Have I touched a sensitive nerve?' Bruno asked mockingly, making no move to go.

'I certainly don't want to be reminded of just how stupid I was to trust you. But at least it taught me never to get emotionally involved with a man again,' Norrie exclaimed bitterly.

Bruno frowned. 'Are you trying to tell me that you haven't been out with another man since then?'

'No, I'm not. I'm just saying that I haven't let myself fall for anyone since. Now will you please go?'

He looked as if he would have liked to ask another question, but changed his mind. 'What about the car?'

'Keep it. I don't want it.'

'No, I'm not going to take it back. Be stubborn if you want to, but it stays here whether you use it or not.' And he dropped the keys on the table. 'Do you have anyone who can baby-sit for you?'

'Why?' Norrie asked, immediately suspicious.

'Do you or don't you?' Bruno said forcefully, his patience wearing thin.

'There is someone I know that I can ask,' Norrie admitted reluctantly. 'But if she isn't free then I have to pay for someone to come from the agency, but they charge so much that I use them as seldom as possible.'

'Contact the agency and ask them to send somebody round tonight. I'll take you out to dinner. Is there any special place where you'd like to eat?'

Norrie gasped indignantly. 'Has it occurred to you that I might not want to go out with you?'

'It has. Which is why I didn't ask.' He smiled suddenly and very devastatingly and said cajolingly, 'Look, we need to talk this over calmly and sensibly, and as we always seem to end up arguing when we're alone, it seems like a good idea to meet in a public place where we won't fly off the handle at each other.'

'There's no guarantee against that even in a restaurant,' Norrie informed him drily.

'You'll come, then. Good. I'll pick you up at seven-thirty. See you.'

And before Norrie could say more than, 'Hey, wait a minute,' he was out of the house and striding off down the road in the direction of the town.

Well, of all the nerve! Norrie watched him go angrily and then slammed the door as she saw one of her neighbours avidly watching from across the road. That was all she needed. Now it would probably be all over the neighbourhood that she was entertaining men in her lunch hour. And when they found out that she'd been given a car as a present ... Norrie suddenly saw the funny side of it and began to giggle and was soon laughing rather hysterically. God, if Bruno only knew what a fool he was making of himself! How I'd love to see his face when he finds out the truth, she thought with malicious enjoyment. But then she sobered just as swiftly as she realised how angry he would be. She shivered for a moment, but then shrugged off the feeling; there was no way he could hurt her, not any more.

Which left the question of whether or not she wanted to go out with him tonight. No, not whether she wanted to, because she most definitely didn't, but it would be extremely amusing to carry on the charade just for a little while longer. Just to see how far Bruno would go in his intention of marrying her of course. She couldn't make up her mind for some time and then decided to leave it to fate. If the agency had a baby-sitter available she would go, but if not she would show Bruno Ben's birth certificate so that he would take his car back and get out of her life again. Reaching for the 'phone she dialled the number.

Bruno knocked on the door promptly at seven-thirty and Norrie opened it, already dressed to go out. His eyebrows rose in pleased surprise as she shut the door behind her. 'I thought I was going to have to fight another battle before you'd come out with me,' he said wryly. Norrie didn't bother to answer and walked past him to his car. He paused before opening the door of the Jaguar for her, his eyes going over her slim figure in the black cocktail dress and sequinned evening jacket, her fair hair in a sleek halo around her head, and her skilfully made up face. 'You look very— sophisticated,' he remarked as he at last opened the door.

'Do I take that as a compliment or not?' she asked coolly when he joined her in the car.

'I'm not even sure myself. You've certainly changed.'

'I'm nearly five years older. And not a girl any more.' She turned to give him a sugar sweet smile. 'But don't worry. You haven't changed a bit. You're still a louse.'

'Thanks,' Bruno smiled grimly. 'Where would you like to eat? I understand there's a good restaurant here in Welford?'

'There is,' Norrie agreed. 'But I'm fussy about whom I'm seen with here, so I'd rather drive to somewhere outside the town, if you don't mind.'

'Are you deliberately trying to provoke me?' Bruno demanded.

'Certainly not,' Norrie replied blandly. 'It comes quite naturally.'

He gave a short bark of laughter. 'This looks as if

it's going to be quite an evening. Well, okay, Norrie, if that's the way you want to play it, it's fine by me.'

They didn't talk again until they arrived at an Italian restaurant in a town to the north of Welford that Norrie hadn't been to before. A word from Bruno and the head waiter placed them at a table for two set in a discreet alcove where they were partly hidden from the rest of the diners.

'Do you still drink sweet sherry as an aperitif?' Bruno asked her as the waiter hovered beside them.

Norrie's eyes widened in surprise at his remembering, but she said coolly, 'No. I'd like a Bacardi and Coke, please.'

Bruno gave the order and turned back to her. 'So your palate has become sophisticated, too, has it?'

'I was extremely young when you knew me.'

'As you said; a girl and not a woman.' His eyes rested on her face and Norrie flushed and looked away, knowing that he was remembering, as she was, the night he had made her a woman.

'And you were right about me having changed,' Norrie said shortly, to break the silence. 'I'm not so gullible now, not so easily taken in by superficial charm.'

'Ouch! That was nasty.'

'It was meant to be.'

It seemed as if they were hell bent for a row anyway, but the waiter innocently prevented it by arriving with the menus and their drinks.

'Cheers,' Bruno said in a sardonic toast. 'Look, can't we call a truce, at least for tonight? This back-biting is getting us absolutely nowhere.'

'*I* don't want to get anywhere,' Norrie pointed out. 'I'm quite happy as I am.' She glanced up and saw him watching her steadily and shrugged. 'Oh, okay.

Have a truce if that's what you want. Although it won't be easy,' she warned.

Bruno gave a small smile and asked her what she would like to eat. For a few minutes they discussed the menu and, because it was a safe subject, it reminded her of the old days when they had gone out together for a meal, when there seemed to be endless things to talk about, to learn about each other. Now, when they'd chosen what they wanted to eat, Norrie couldn't think of a thing to say, so she covered it by looking round the restaurant.

'Have you been here before?' Bruno asked.

'No, but I've heard about it. It has a good reputation.'

'Where do your dates usually take you?'

Norrie looked at him quickly, wondering if he was insinuating anything, but his face was quite bland. 'Around.'

'Have you a boyfriend at the moment?'

She shook her head. 'No one in particular.'

'And you haven't been tempted to settle down since—since we last met?'

'Once bitten, twice shy,' she answered drily. 'And it may be an old cliché but it still holds true.'

'So you haven't had a—shall we say relationship, with anyone since me?'

'I didn't say that,' Norrie pointed out sardonically. 'Anyway I don't for a second suppose that you've led a celibate life for the last four and a half years.'

Bruno gave a short laugh. 'Hardly. But I would be sorry to think that what happened between us has put you off men.'

'It hasn't put me off men,' Norrie said sweetly. 'Just off trusting them.'

'I see.' Bruno looked down at his glass, a rather

bleak look in his dark eyes. 'Do you think you might have got married—if it hadn't been for Ben?'

Norrie was tempted to try and make him feel guilty by saying yes, but she shook her head. 'No, I haven't met anyone I cared about enough to even contemplate it.'

'So there's nothing to stop you marrying me?'

'Only the fact that I don't want to,' she told him calmly.

Bruno smiled and changed the subject. 'How long have you been working for the *Observer*?'

'A couple of years. But you must know that already, you had all the personnel files to look at before we even knew you were taking the paper over. So you knew I was here.'

'Yes,' he admitted. 'It came as quite a surprise to see your name on the list.'

'But you still came here to handle things yourself. Couldn't you have sent someone else?'

'It wasn't something I cared to delegate.' He paused, then added rather brusquely, 'And maybe I wanted to see you again.'

'Why? Because you thought it might be amusing to see if you could still attract me, was that it?' she demanded bitterly.

Bruno's hand reached out and covered hers as it lay on the table, gripping hard. 'No,' he said forcefully. 'It was never that. I wanted to see you because I've always been sad that we parted the way we did, on such bad terms. I wanted to see if we could—patch things up, and at least be friends. But you made it perfectly obvious that you didn't want to know, so I was willing to leave it at that, until I found out about Ben.' For a moment anger showed in his eyes and his grip hurt so that she gasped and he abruptly let go of her hand. 'I'm sorry, I didn't mean to hurt you. I suppose it was my fault that you didn't tell me about Ben. I should have made sure that you were okay before we split up.'

Norrie slid her hand under the table. 'Here's our food,' she said brightly as the waiter came up. 'I'm starving, aren't you?' Adding rather desperately, 'Where do you live now?'

'In London. I have a flat near Regent's Park, and at the moment I'm commuting from there to Welford every day. It hasn't got a garden unfortunately, but the park is only a short walk away. And Ben will enjoy being able to go to the zoo.'

'You seem to take it for granted that I'm going to fall in with your plans.'

'Why not? If you look at it purely from the financial aspect, you'll be getting a pretty good bargain. Security for yourself and Ben for the rest of your life, companionship, a home in London, anything you want that I can give you.'

'And you,' Norrie added sardonically.

'And me,' he agreed.

'And just what do you expect in return for all these riches?'

He refilled her glass with wine while he considered it. 'First and foremost of course to be able to have my son with me, and to have a say in his upbringing.' His eyes challenged hers but Norrie didn't speak. So he went on, 'And to have you.' Her eyebrows rose at that and he tagged on mockingly, 'To take care of Ben and to act as hostess when I entertain. In short, to be a wife.'

Norrie tilted her head to one side and pretended to consider his offer, then shook her head. 'Sorry, but I prefer to be on my own in a hovel in Welford than live with you in your concrete palace.'

'So if you don't like it we'll find a house somewhere. I only live there because it's convenient for my office, but I understand that a kid needs a garden, and I don't mind commuting from wherever you want to live.'

'How about Devon?' Norrie suggested sarcastically.

His face grew grim. 'If you had wanted to stay in Devon, you would never have left.' A thought occurred to him. 'Unless you left there because of Ben. Because you didn't want anyone to know.'

Honestly, he was almost asking to be fooled, the way he was playing into her hands. Norrie didn't answer, letting him think that he was right, and instead made some comment about the food. Bruno accepted the change of topic and told her about some of the eating places he'd visited on trips abroad and in London.

'You eat out a lot?' she asked.

'Most of the time. Occasionally I cook for myself but it's quicker and easier to go to a restaurant. And when I have clients to entertain I always take them out to lunch or dinner.'

'Our lives appear to be complete opposites. Ben's big treat is to share a Chinese takeaway.'

Bruno laughed. 'I can imagine.' He beckoned the waiter over and ordered another bottle of wine. 'But I'm sure we're not all that different. We certainly weren't once,' he reminded her softly.

Norrie judged it wisest to ignore that remark and concentrated on finishing her pudding. 'That was delicious.'

'I'm glad you enjoyed it. Would you like coffee?'

'Please. But if you'll excuse me for a few minutes I think I'll just 'phone to make sure that Ben is all right.'

'Is he unwell?' Bruno asked sharply.

'I'd hardly have left him if he was,' Norrie retorted,

rather resenting the anxious note in his voice. 'I just want to check, that's all.'

But the baby-sitter reported that Ben was still fast asleep, and after applying fresh lipstick in the cloakroom, Norrie returned to their table.

A small group had been playing softly in the background, but now that most people had finished their meal they began to play more up-beat numbers and several couples got up to dance. Bruno stood up as she rejoined him and put a hand on her arm before she sat down. 'Would you like to dance?'

'You must be joking!' Norrie retorted in surprise.

'Of course I'm not. Don't be such a coward.' And he put a firm arm round her waist and propelled her on to the floor.

Short of making an embarrassing scene, there wasn't much Norrie could do except go along with him, but her face was angry as she turned and he drew her to him and began to move around the floor. 'You know darn well that I don't want to dance with you.' But Bruno ignored her. 'Must you hold me so close?' she demanded crossly.

He bent his head and said softly into her ear, 'Relax. What are you afraid of?'

But she held herself stiffly in his arms, automatically moving to the music, but terribly aware of his hand low on her back, of the musky tang of his after-shave, of the length of his body close against hers, of his mouth only a few inches away. How could she possibly relax when his nearness aroused her so. And he knew it, too, damn him. Bruno felt her hand tremble in his and he gave a slow smile, then let his lips lightly brush her temple.

'You're very lovely,' he said softly. 'You always were.'

'Shut up. I don't want to hear.'

He laughed softly. 'Little liar. There isn't a woman in the world who doesn't like having compliments paid her.'

'That depends entirely on who's paying them,' Norrie pointed out tartly. 'Coming from you they're—they're odious.'

His grip tightened suddenly and he pulled her hard against him, an angry glitter in his eyes. And he held her pressed close to him, so that she could feel every movement of his hips, until the music ended.

Her face flaming, Norrie strode off the dance floor as soon as he let her go, picked up her bag from the table and would have walked out if Bruno hadn't caught her elbow and forced her to sit down. 'Drink your coffee,' he ordered.

'I don't want it.'

'Don't be so damn childish.'

'How dare you—handle me like that?'

'You were rude once too often. And we agreed to call a truce, if you remember.'

Norrie glared at him, hating him because he still had the power to arouse her. 'I *knew* it was a mistake to come out with you.'

'Why? Because you found out that you're not so immune to me as you like to think you are?'

'Rubbish. You don't even turn me on any more.'

'No?' He reached out again and captured her hand. 'Then why is your hand trembling?'

'It isn't trembling, it's—it's shaking with anger,' Norrie retorted, snatching it away.

Bruno laughed. 'You'll have to put up a more convincing performance than that before I'll even start to believe you.'

'Well, it's true. Okay, I fell for you once, but that

doesn't mean that you can just walk back into my life and take it over, or expect me to feel the same way about you. We're different people now, and sexually you leave me cold.'

His eyes narrowed. 'Prove it.'

'What?' Norrie stared at him, her imagination running wild.

He laughed softly at her expression. 'I don't mean any—er—shall we say total commitment? I just meant prove it by—dancing with me again.'

'Oh, really, that's ridiculous. You know I don't . . .'

'Scared?' he demanded, his dark eyes challenging.

'No, I'm not scared. I just don't see any point in it, that's all. Why can't you just accept my word for it that I find you repulsive? I don't mind repeating it until it finally sinks in,' she added nastily.

'Stop trying to sidetrack me. If you're not scared then come and dance again.'

Norrie looked across at him exasperatedly. 'Oh, okay, if that's what it will take to convince you.' And she stood up and walked ahead of him on to the floor.

The group were playing another slow, smoochy number. The lights were turned down low and there were already several couples on the floor, holding each other close, made amorous by the food and wine.

Bruno took her in his arms and Norrie tried to relax and keep control of her emotions, his other hand holding hers against his chest. He moved slowly, only a few inches at a time, so that the closeness of his body hardly left her. Norrie was careful not to look at him, keeping her eyes firmly fixed over his shoulder, but after they'd been dancing for a few minutes and she'd started to congratulate herself on her self-control, an old memory suddenly stirred in her heart and it seemed as if the years in between had never been. She closed her eyes tightly, trying to shut it out and her steps faltered. Bruno glanced quickly down at her and drew her against him, her head on his shoulder. A tear gathered and ran down her cheek and he bent to gently kiss it away.

'Sweetheart,' he said softly. 'I know. I know.'

Her hand moved convulsively in his and he held it tightly. She made a small muffled sound, almost of pain, as the sweet memories and feelings flooded back, and he put his face against hers, his lips soft on her skin. Norrie quivered, her emotions raw, and let him hold her, all resistance lost in the depth of emotion her memories evoked, but after a few minutes he led her off the floor, his arm supporting her as he collected her bag and they left the restaurant.

His car was parked nearby and he helped her into it, not speaking until he had driven a few miles and turned off the main road into a quiet lay-by that overlooked the lights of the town. Switching off the engine, Bruno turned to look at her as she rested her head against the window, her eyes still wet with tears.

'Darling.' He undid her safety belt and reached to draw her to him, softly kissing her eyelids, the line of her cheek, and hovering at the corner of her mouth, touching her lips but not quite kissing them. 'Don't try and hide it, not any more,' he murmured against her mouth. 'Cry if you want to.'

He put a hand in her hair, releasing it from its clip and then his lips were on her throat, his breath hot and sensuous against her skin, so that she gasped and gripped his shoulders, tilting her head back as his lips travelled along the column of her neck. 'Bruno . . .'

'Hush,' he whispered. 'Don't talk.' Raising his head a little, he gently bit her ear lobe, sending a violent quiver of desire shooting through her body.

A small, animal moan escaped her and Norrie slowly turned her head to meet his mouth. He took her lips hungrily, triumphantly, hurting her with the intensity of his kiss. But she welcomed the pain, returning his embrace with a long-forgotten fervour, losing herself in his arms with a greedy passion that had too long been starved of fulfilment. His hands were on either side of her face, holding her captive beneath his kiss, but presently, as their breathing became ragged, he moved his right hand down and pushed her jacket off her shoulders and then the straps of her dress.

For a moment she stiffened and made a sound of protest, but then his hand was on her breast and she gave a cry of sensuous delight. It had been so long, so long. Her body ached as he caressed her, his experienced fingers lightly toying with her until her hardened nipple betrayed her body's pleasure.

'You're beautiful,' he whispered. 'Beautiful.' And lowered his head to replace his fingers with his lips.

Norrie gave a long, groaning sigh of sensual delight and twined her fingers in his hair, holding his head against her, his caress driving her mad with frustrated yearning. His lips pulled at her, bit gently until she couldn't stand it any longer and had to tear herself away. She covered herself with her hands and stared at him, her breath rasping and ragged. She couldn't speak, could only gaze at him with wide, astonished eyes, her mouth parted sensuously.

Bruno pushed his hair back from his forehead, his dark eyes running over her. 'Come here,' he said softly.

'No.' But his eyes held hers and she slowly moved towards him.

'Show me,' he commanded, his eyes lowered, and after a few moments' hesitation she reluctantly moved her hands to bare her breasts to his greedy eyes. He cupped them in his hands and bent to kiss them again. 'They're mine. And you're mine,' he told her and took her mouth in fierce male arrogance, with a domination that couldn't be denied.

At last he let her go and lifted the straps of her dress, covering her himself instead of letting Norrie do it, a gesture which was so dismissive that she felt like a doll that someone had finished playing with and put aside. He started the car and began to drive back to Welford while Norrie tried to tidy her hair with hands that trembled uncontrollably. Bruno glanced at her, a small smile curving his lips as he saw that she was still shaken by emotion.

When they drew up outside the cottage he said, 'Stay here. I'll pay off the baby-sitter.' And Norrie was infinitely grateful for that; she couldn't have borne to be seen in this state, with her hair loose and smudged make-up. They would tell their own story even without the added evidence of her shaking hands and the awakened sensuality in her face.

Bruno saw the baby-sitter away and then came for her, his firm hand supporting her as she half-walked, half-stumbled inside. He closed the door and leant against it, watching her as she turned to face him. 'I want you,' he told her clearly. 'I want to take you to bed and make love to you again.'

For a long moment Norrie could only gaze at him, but then she closed her eyes, fighting for some degree of sanity. And being in the cottage helped: she thought of Ben lying asleep in his room upstairs, of her own room that Bruno wanted to invade—that and her body. But the room was hers alone, as was this house, and her body, too. Nothing would ever be the same if she let him stay, if she let him destroy her life again.

She would feel cheap and dirty for the rest of her life. Opening her eyes, Norrie shook her head. 'No. Not here, not now.'

Swiftly he strode across and put his hands on her arms. 'Why not? You want it as much as I do. You know you do.'

'No. I—I can't. Please Bruno.' She tried to move away but he wouldn't let her.

'Stop trying to fight me,' he said impatiently. 'What more proof do you need that you're still mine, that you still love me?' He kissed her suddenly, his hands low on her hips, holding her against the growing hardness of his body, letting her know how much he wanted her.

But it was his arrogant possessiveness that somehow replaced desire with cold hatred again. As she realised how weak she'd been, how she'd fallen into his arms, Norrie was filled with almost physical revulsion. And even as he kissed her, she was trying to think of some way she could get her own back, some way she could prove to him once and for all that she was still in control of her own feelings. And as he let her go and smiled down at her, sure that he'd won, an idea came to her for a way that she could get her own back for everything he'd ever done to her. But hadn't it always been there, at the back of her mind, ever since he'd thought that Ben was his and asked her to marry him? But before it had only been a fleeting thought that she had hardly dared to dwell on, now, suddenly, she knew, with certainty, that she was going to carry it through.

Acting for all she was worth, she smiled up at him and put her arms around his neck. 'Yes, of course I want you. I want you very much. But it just isn't—well, convenient at the moment. And besides,' she moved her hips provocatively against his, 'I only have a single bed. And the walls of this house are very thin.'

'When and where, then?' he said huskily, his hands gripping her.

'Where, that's up to you. And when? Well, we'll have all the time in the world, won't we?'

Bruno caught his breath. 'You mean you'll marry me?'

She laughed and didn't have to pretend the shake in her voice. 'There doesn't really seem any reason not to, does there? Not if we're going to make love anyway.'

'Norrie,' he breathed. 'My darling girl. I swear you won't regret it. There's so much I want to say to you, to tell you. I've waited so long to . . .'

But Norrie put a hand over his mouth, not wanting to hear, afraid that her resolve might be weakened. 'Not now,' she whispered. 'Tell me on—on our wedding day.'

'When? When will you marry me?'

Reaching up she kissed him softly on the mouth. 'You said three weeks, didn't you? There's nothing to wait for, is there?'

There was a blaze of surprised happiness in his eyes as Bruno said, 'No, nothing. Not if you're sure.'

'Oh, I'm quite sure. But—let's talk about it some other time, shall we? Tonight there's been too much excitement, and too much wine probably, and I'm very tired.'

'All right. I'll 'phone you tomorrow.' He kissed her again and now the possessiveness was so obvious that Norrie had to make a conscious effort not to let her feelings show on her face. But Bruno was so sure of his triumph that he didn't notice anything, thank goodness. 'I can't wait to take you to bed,' he murmured against her mouth. 'I want you so much.'

Norrie pretended to laugh and pushed him towards the door. 'Go home. It's getting late, and we'll both have lots to do tomorrow.'

He grinned down at her, supremely confident, and sure now that she was his to take whenever he wanted. 'All right, I'll go. Sleep well, darling. Dream about me.'

'I'll try.' She smiled at him mistily. 'But somehow I don't think I'm going to sleep much tonight.'

Bruno laughed and kissed her again before reluctantly turning to go at last. Norrie stood dutifully in the doorway to watch him go but, as soon as he'd turned the corner, slammed the door and ran upstairs to the bathroom, pulling off her clothes and scrubbing herself clean where he'd touched her until her skin was red and sore. Tears ran down her cheeks, tears of self-hatred and humiliation. How could she have lost her senses so easily? She must be mad, mad! But God, she'd pay him back! She'd make him wish he'd never set eyes on her. Staring at her reflection in the mirror, Norrie swore that she'd never let him get to her again, and that Bruno would live to more than regret that he'd ever met her.

CHAPTER SIX

THEY were married just over three weeks later in a simple and short ceremony in a Registrar's office in the town nearby. They could have been married in Welford, but Norrie had stipulated the town because she didn't want anyone from the *Observer* to know that she was marrying a man she'd told them she hated. For the same reason, she hadn't invited anyone she knew to the wedding, and as neither of them had any close relations they had to use two of the Registrar's clerks as witnesses.

At first Bruno had wanted to have a reception afterwards, but Norrie had persuaded him to wait until they were settled and then give a party to celebrate. He had agreed willingly enough, especially when she mentioned that Ben got sick with excitement for days before a party and they certainly wouldn't get any sleep the night after it. Ben, she found, could be used as a good excuse for getting her way in most things; she even used him to keep Bruno at arm's length during the three weeks leading up to the wedding by insisting that they couldn't make love at the cottage because the walls were so thin that Ben would hear and might be frightened. And when Bruno booked a hotel room the following weekend the baby-sitter had 'unfortunately' let her down at the last minute so that Norrie couldn't go to him. And after that it hadn't been too difficult to coax him into waiting until after the wedding. 'Think how much nicer it will be when we're relaxed and have plenty of time,' she'd whispered to him.

Bruno had groaned, but waiting had added an extra layer of spice to anticipation, and by promising him future total surrender she had managed to withhold it for the time being. But she hadn't been able to escape his love-making completely; as a promise of better things to come, she had several times had to let him pull her down on to his lap and return his kisses while he undid her blouse and bra and caressed her as much as he wanted. And it had been all too appallingly easy to lie in his arms and let his hands and lips work their erotic magic on her senses, only some small core of her mind retaining its hold on sanity and holding her back from pleading with him to take her now—now.

But somehow she had survived until the wedding, and they had been very busy of course; Bruno had brought in one of his employees to take over from him at the *Welford Observer* and oversee the introduction of the new editions, so that he would be free for the holiday-cum-honeymoon that he insisted they take. And Norrie had found plenty to do sorting out her own and Ben's belongings, deciding what she wanted to take with her and what to leave behind, only it was difficult when she wasn't sure how long they would be away. Bruno had told her to put her cottage up for sale and she had lied and said she had put it in the hands of an estate agent, but in reality had only told the nursery school and everyone else concerned that she was going to stay with relatives for a few weeks. She would need the cottage again when she finally told Bruno the truth and he threw them out.

In those three weeks Bruno never came to the house empty-handed, there was usually a present for Norrie and always something for Ben, who began to think it

was Christmas every day and ran eagerly to greet
Bruno whenever the Jaguar pulled up outside. He
doted on the boy and wanted him to call him Daddy of
course, but Norrie got round that by saying it would
be embarrassing for her while they were still in
Welford and to wait until they'd moved to London.
She was afraid that Ben would be spoilt by all the toys,
and not able to understand it when later the presents
suddenly stopped, so she told Bruno not to bring the
child something every time. He looked rueful, 'Sorry.
I suppose I'm making up for all the years I've missed,'
he admitted from where he was sitting on the floor
showing Ben how to put together a spaceship he'd
brought him. He got to his feet and handed her a
package. 'Maybe you'll let me spoil you instead.'

Slowly Norrie unwrapped the parcel and opened a
box which contained a gorgeous cream silk nightdress
with thin straps and beautifully delicate lace around
the low-cut top and up the slits in the side which
reached almost to the waist. And with it was a
matching négligé. 'Why—why they're beautiful.' She
slid her hand inside the nightdress and ran it along the
satin smoothness of the silk.

'Wear them on our wedding night,' he said softly,
his hands on her shoulders as he stood behind her.

'Yes. All right.'

He turned her to face him and bent to kiss her, but
had hardly put his mouth to hers before Ben was
between them, pushing at Bruno's legs. 'Leave Norrie
'lone. Leave Norrie 'lone.'

Bruno laughed and bent to swing Ben up on to his
shoulders. 'We're going to have to cure him of this
jealousy—and fast.'

Norrie had laughed, too, but in relief, hoping that
Ben would keep up his possessive attitude at least for a

few more weeks. It was hard enough to keep up her own attitude; she didn't sleep much that night, not that she had slept very much since she had been crazy enough to say that she would marry Bruno, and her conscience hit her every time she thought about it. A dozen times a day she wanted to back out, and had even got as far as starting a letter to tell him so, because there was no way she could face him with it, but he came to the house so often, as if he was afraid she might change her mind and was determined to prevent it. And while he was there his possessiveness towards both Ben and herself and the arrogant way he took it for granted that she must still be in love with him, brought back all the deep feelings of antagonism that allowed her to keep up the charade. It was only when she was alone, lying awake far into the night, that she wondered what on earth she was getting herself into.

The wedding day had come at last, all too fast and yet in some ways infinitely slowly. Bruno had arranged for the agency to send someone round quite early so that Norrie would have time to get ready in peace, and he had insisted on giving her the money to buy herself an outfit for the wedding and clothes for their honeymoon, so she had bought a pale blue suit with a short, fitted jacket and straight skirt, a high-necked white silk blouse with a matching bow, and a pretty little hat with a veil that covered her eyes. At eleven the gold Jaguar pulled up outside and Norrie nervously picked up her bag and gloves. The baby-sitter had taken Ben into the kitchen and Norrie slipped quickly out of the house before he could start making a fuss and demand to go with her.

Bruno had just unlatched the gate but he paused when he saw her, his eyes running over her

admiringly. 'I'm always overwhelmed by how sophisticated you can look now.' He opened the door of the
car for her and turned to look at her again as soon as
he joined her, then picked up her hand and turned it
over to gently kiss her palm. 'You look very, very
lovely.'

'Thank you. But not here, please. I'm sure everyone
is looking at us.' And she pulled her hand away and
quickly put on her gloves.

'A bride should expect to be looked at on her
wedding day,' Bruno teased.

'But hardly in these circumstances. Let's go, please.'

He started the car and drove out of Welford,
glancing at her as they travelled along the by-pass to
say, 'Nervous?'

'Yes, I suppose I am, rather,' Norrie admitted. 'It
all feels totally unreal, like a dream. I keep expecting
to wake up at any moment and find that you never
came to Welford, never took over the Observer.'

Bruno laughed. 'But this is one dream that's going
to go on forever.'

Only it will soon become a nightmare for you,
Norrie thought as she looked at him. He was wearing a
beautifully tailored pale grey suit that looked new. It
fitted him well, emphasising the width of his shoulders
and the athletic slimness of his waist. His hair had
been professionally washed and his hands manicured.
He looked what he was, a successful executive
businessman who was still on his way up, ambitious,
capable and supremely confident. He also looked
arrogantly masculine, handsome, and somehow exuded
sex appeal without having to do a thing about it. And
he looked very happy. Well, let him while he could,
she would soon stab his conceited pride.

Soon they drew up outside the Registrar's Office

and Bruno leant over to the back seat. 'Perhaps this will make you feel more like a bride,' he suggested, and handed her a bouquet of pale yellow rosebuds and stephanotis. 'Remember I gave you yellow roses once before,' he reminded her softly.

Norrie remembered all right; it had been the night he had first made love to her, when he had taken her to his flat and she had been so nervous that she had dropped the flowers on the floor and they hadn't been picked up until the next morning. For a moment she buried her face in the flowers, giving herself time to control her features, and then turned to him with a brittle smile. 'How wonderful of you to remember.'

'I remember everything about those months,' he told her softly. 'Norrie, I've been wanting to say this to you ever since I saw you again, I . . .'

'Oh, look at the time! Oughtn't we to go in? We don't want to be late.'

Norrie's exclamation interrupted him and Bruno looked rueful, but he fixed a carnation in his buttonhole and then escorted her into the Registrar's Office. They were early of course and had to sit in the waiting room for nearly ten minutes before they were shown in and the ceremony began. It was a small and rather bare room, with just a desk, some chairs for the witnesses and a big safe over in the corner. It was all over very quickly and afterwards Norrie couldn't remember a word of the promises she'd made. All she could recall was the strength in Bruno's hands as he'd slid a ring on to her finger, and the shock of realisation when the Registrar had called her Mrs Denton and handed her the marriage certificate.

From then onwards Norrie seemed to be two people: the one who acted and responded like any normal woman, and the other who watched herself in a kind of daze and wondered how the hell she'd got herself into this mess.

Bruno took her for a celebration lunch to the best restaurant in town and they shared a bottle of champagne, which didn't help. She was so nervous that she got a bit giggly in the car afterwards, which Bruno seemed to find very amusing. He tried to kiss her but she pretended to tease him. 'Behave yourself.'

'We *are* married,' he pointed out, reaching for her again.

'That's the point; married people behave respectably. They don't neck in cars.' And she playfully eluded his hands.

'Where do they neck, then?'

But she was ready for that one. 'They don't. They give each other a passing peck on the cheek first thing in the morning and last thing at night.'

'I don't think I'm going to like being married if I'm going to be rationed to two pecks on the cheek per day.'

'You should have thought of that yesterday when you were an irresponsible playboy,' Norrie retorted. 'Come on, Ben's waiting for us.'

Bruno put a finger under her chin and smiled into her eyes. 'Remind me to tell you how crazy I am about you later.'

Norrie's heart began to beat wildly, as if it was all for real and not a dangerous game of retaliation. 'You mean, later—when you get your peck on the cheek?'

He laughed and covered her hand, squeezing it. 'Most definitely.'

They drove back to the cottage and picked up Ben and the luggage, and then headed for the coast. Bruno had had a child's seat fitted into the back of the Jaguar, which Ben thought was great because he could see out of the windows. Norrie turned in her seat to watch his puzzled little face while Bruno told him that they were going to the seaside, and tried to explain that they were now married and Ben could call him Daddy. Ben, it went without saying, asked an awful lot of questions but Norrie sat silently, letting Bruno answer them and ignoring the somewhat startled and agonised looks he gave her at some of Ben's questions.

'Emma at school said her Daddy and Mummy go to sleep in the same bed,' Ben told them.

'That's right,' Bruno answered, pleased they'd got that sorted out.

'I go in Norrie's bed when there's a big noise in the sky.'

Bruno raised an eyebrow and Norrie said helpfully, 'He means a thunderstorm.'

'Oh. Well, that's all right, old son. You can still come in with us and we'll both look after you. You won't be frightened then.'

'*I* not frightened. *Norrie's* frightened,' Ben exclaimed indignantly. 'I have to give Norrie cuddle, not you. You sleep in my bed.'

For a lovely moment Bruno looked completely taken aback but then he recovered magnificently and said firmly, 'Mummies and Daddies have to sleep in the same bed, it's the law.' But he hastily changed the subject. 'Now I'll tell you about this seaside place we're going to.'

He had booked a suite in a five-star hotel on the coast only a couple of hours' drive from Welford, because Ben wasn't used to long car journeys and Norrie didn't want him to get over-excited and tired, but he was so eager to see the sea that he clamoured to be taken down to the beach as soon as they arrived.

'I'll take him while you unpack, if you like?' Bruno

offered, and was gone for over an hour. When they came back Ben was tired out and Bruno was carrying him against his shoulder. He very gently moved him and held him in his arms a moment, his eyes full of pride and tenderness as he looked down at the child.

As Norrie turned to take Ben from him she saw his face and knew suddenly that whatever else she did to him, finding out that Ben wasn't his was going to hurt Bruno the most, that his love for the boy he thought was his son was already deeper than anything he had ever felt for her—or any woman if it came to that.

'I'd better take him down for some food before he falls asleep.'

The hotel had a room set aside for young children and there were several other parents there, feeding their offspring, which made Ben perk up a bit and he ate hungrily, but was glad enough when Norrie took him upstairs again and gave him his bath. By then Bruno had had his own bath and changed ready for dinner, but came with her when she took Ben into the smaller bedroom of the suite, watching as she tucked him in and gave him a goodnight kiss.

'Would you like me to read to him or something while you change?' Bruno offered diffidently.

He was being very tactful, Norrie realised, not wanting her to think that he was trying to take Ben over. She smiled and nodded. 'Thanks, that would be a help.'

Glancing back at the door, she saw Bruno sit on the bed and put an arm round Ben while he sorted out a story book. It seemed incongruous, somehow, and she couldn't reconcile the ruthless man that she knew Bruno to be with the gentleness he was showing to Ben. He looked up and, as if guessing something of her thoughts, grinned rather ruefully, 'I've an idea this is doing nothing for my image.'

'On the contrary,' Norrie said lightly, and left him to it. She took her time in the bathroom, having a leisurely bath scented with the bubble bath that the hotel provided, and carefully redoing her hair and make-up. There had been enough to buy several dresses with the money that Bruno had given her, and she had chosen a pale green one to wear tonight, one that had full sleeves but was cut low at the front and clung to her hips before swirling out into a full skirt. She added a generous helping of scent at all her pulse points and took a long, slow look at herself. The effects of the champagne had worn off by now and she felt remarkably cool and clear-headed, not in the least nervous and ready to play this game to its first confrontation.

He was sitting in an armchair reading a magazine when Norrie finally came out of the bathroom. Putting the paper down, Bruno let his eyes run slowly over her, making no attempt to hide his desire as they rested on the curves of her hips and then her breasts. Standing up, he crossed the room to stand beside her. 'That was well worth the wait,' he said softly and bent to kiss her, but Norrie moved her head away.

'You'll mess up my lipstick.'

He rested his hands on her waist. 'I'm beginning to think you've become a tease.'

'Of course.' She rotated her hips so that her thighs moved against his.

He groaned. 'Minx. Let's forget about dinner and go to bed now.'

'And waste all the time I've spent getting ready?' She pushed him away. 'Besides, I'm hungry.'

'Okay, you win.' But she could tell by the way he

said it that he was only indulging her teasing because he knew that his time to take her would soon come.

As they were shown to their table in the dining-room, many heads turned to look at them, both male and female, and Norrie wondered if anyone guessed that this was their wedding day. But how could they when they had Ben with them? And yet she caught several eyes watching them when she looked round. 'We seem to be the centre of attention,' she murmured as they sat down.

'Why not? The men are all thinking how lucky I am.'

Norrie looked at him demurely. 'And the women?'

He grinned and gave a mock leer. 'They're probably being as catty as hell about you to hide their jealousy.'

'And why should they be jealous of me?'

'Because they'd like to be in your place, of course.'

'I see you have no illusions of false modesty to worry about.'

His eyes crinkled. 'Well you should know.'

Norrie flushed. 'I think we'd better look at the menu,' she said primly and looked away from his amused laughter.

There was no dance floor in the dining-room, nothing to keep them there once the meal was finished. Norrie delayed as much as she could, but the service was all too efficient and the meal was finished within a couple of hours.

'Would you like to have another coffee or a liqueur in the lounge?' Bruno suggested. Norrie accepted with relief, although she caught a flash of amusement in his eyes as though he knew she was prevaricating.

'I'll just go up and make sure that Ben's okay first,' and she left him to make his own way to the lounge.

Ben was fast asleep but had kicked off all his covers,

as he did every night. Norrie tucked him in again and gently brushed his fair hair out of his eyes. For the first time it occurred to her that she was involving Ben in something in which he was going to be nothing but an innocent pawn. And life with Bruno, after tonight, wasn't going to be exactly a bed of roses. Ben might be hurt by it, or at the very least unsettled. But it was too late now, she couldn't go back, although for a few minutes she was tempted to just pick up Ben and run. But she was committed now, and her hatred of Bruno was deep enough for her to hesitate only a few seconds before she dismissed all thoughts of the consequences from her mind; she'd wanted to hurt him and it was just about to begin.

He was waiting for her in the lounge, sitting on a small settee with brandy balloons and cups of coffee on a low table in front of him. 'Is he okay?' he asked as she joined him. 'You seemed to be rather a long time.'

'Yes, he was fine.' It was only a small seat so she had to sit close beside him and Bruno didn't move up to make more room for her.

Picking up the glasses, he gave one to her before clinking them gently together. 'My last toast of the evening,' he said, looking into her eyes. 'To my very lovely bride.'

Norrie smiled back at him, feeling strangely cool and resolved now that the time was almost here. 'I think you already made that one during dinner,' she pointed out.

'A good thing can't be repeated too often.'

'Can't it?' she pouted softly, looking at him under her lashes. She could feel the warmth of his thigh next to hers and deliberately moved in her seat, then leant forward so that her breast brushed his arm.

'Hurry up and drink your brandy,' he commanded.

'Don't be silly, one never hurries over brandy.' But she raised the glass to her lips and provocatively slid her tongue along its rim.

'Do you know what you're doing to me?' Bruno demanded huskily.

'No. What?'

'Let's go to bed.'

'It's too early. It's not even ten-thirty yet.'

'Good, that will give us more time.'

Norrie gave a small smile and turned to look round the lounge feeling a dizzy kind of power at this cat and mouse game she was playing; and Bruno was rushing headlong towards his own fate, because as he reached to take the bait, the trap would spring.

After a couple of minutes, she moved her free hand and deliberately placed it on his leg, a few inches above his knee. Putting down her glass, she leant her head back against the settee and turned to face him. He did the same, his head only a few inches away from hers, and her heart gave a jerk at the tenderness in his eyes.

'I like that scent you're wearing.'

'Thank you.' She moved her fingers, gently stroking them along the inside of his leg.

He gave a small gasp and she knew that the caress, in such a public place, was turning him on. He stood it for a few minutes then hastily captured her hand. 'Do you really want that coffee?'

Norrie shook her head. 'No.'

'Then for God's sake let's go to bed! You're driving me crazy.'

They had to walk decorously through the lounge and nod good night to the receptionist before climbing the stairs to their suite on the first floor. Bruno fitted the key into the lock and tried to grab her as soon as they were inside and the door shut, but Norrie laughed and held him away. 'Don't you want me to change into that nightdress you bought me?'

'Who needs it?' he said thickly, pulling her close and kissing her neck.

'No. Come on, we have to do this properly.' She pushed him away. 'You can change in the bedroom while I use the bathroom.'

'Save the nightdress for tomorrow night.' His hands went to the zip at the back of her dress and began to pull it down. 'I want to undress you and . . .'

'No, tonight's our wedding night. Please, Bruno; you said you wanted me to feel like a bride.'

He straightened up and nodded. 'All right, but if you're not out of there in ten minutes . . .'

She laughed. 'You'll break the door down. Okay, I get the message.' Going into the bedroom, Norrie slipped off her dress and hung it up, then collected her night things and went into the bathroom. She changed as quickly as Bruno could have wanted, but took time over brushing her hair so that it hung in shining silken waves on her shoulders, then added more scent before pirouetting in front of the mirror to note how the nightdress clung to her, covering her body but revealing the soft curve of her breasts, the slimness of her waist and taut flatness of her stomach, and on down the long length of her thighs and legs. Yes, she would do. She wanted Bruno to know exactly what he was missing.

Norrie grew still suddenly, staring at herself in the mirror, the enormity of what she was about to do making her tremble with sick fear now that the moment had arrived. She couldn't go through with it, she couldn't! She would just have to tell Bruno the truth and beg him to forgive her. Turning, she put her hand on the door knob, intending to go out and confess everything, but her hand was shaking so much that she fumbled with the catch, and those few seconds made her pause as she pictured what would happen. He wouldn't forgive her, no way. And he didn't have any mercy in his make-up; he had already proved that. He would just use her weakness to do what he wanted to her, and then kick them out. And the hell of pretending during these last weeks would all have been for nothing. It was too late; to back down now would be even worse than going through with it. For a few moments Norrie leaned her head against the door, wishing herself anywhere but here, but then turned with a hopeless kind of determination to finish getting ready.

She put on the négligé just as he rapped impatiently on the door. 'The ten minutes are up.'

Deciding to leave the négligé untied, Norrie switched off the light and slowly opened the door to stand framed in the doorway, one leg forward of the other so that he could better see its slender curve.

Bruno turned as she opened the door and stood staring at her for a long moment. 'You were right,' he said slowly. 'Tonight is very, very special.' Then, thickly, 'Come here, Mrs Denton.'

Norrie looked at him and smiled a little, but moved slowly to obey him. He was wearing only a pair of pyjamas, the top unbuttoned, and it was already obvious that he wanted her. Drawing her into his arms, he kissed her, his hand in her hair, taking all the time in the world about it, his lips soft and sensuous, not yet yielding to passion. Then he let her go and reached up to take off her négligé, letting it slip off her shoulders to lie in silken confusion at her feet. 'I love you, my darling,' he said with soft sincerity. 'I've always loved you.'

'Do you?' Norrie looked up into his face, her own quite expressionless.

Thinking that she doubted him, Bruno said forcefully, 'I swear it!'

'Good. I'm glad. That makes it all the better.' Then she stepped back from him. 'I'm going to bed.'

He gave a slightly surprised grin. 'I know.'

'Alone,' Norrie said coldly. Not understanding, he gave a small laugh and reached for her again, but she knocked his arm away. 'Don't touch me.'

Bruno frowned. 'What is it? What's the matter, darling?'

'You heard me,' she said clearly, 'I'm going to bed—alone. You can sleep in the spare bed in Ben's room.'

She moved to walk away but Bruno caught her arm and spun her round. 'Hey, the time for teasing's over.' Then he saw the cold hatred in her face. 'But I see you're not teasing,' he said slowly, his features changing from surprise to growing wariness.

'No. I'm not.'

'So just what is this?'

'I should have thought that was obvious. You wanted to marry me for Ben's sake. Well, you've done that. But that's *all* you're getting. There are no—conjugal rights, or whatever you care to call it, included in the package deal.'

Bruno stared at her, still holding her arm. 'Are you jealous because of Ben? Do you think I only married you to get him? But it isn't so.' He caught hold of her other shoulder. 'I've just told you that I've always loved you. Okay, giving Ben my name was important to me, but he was an excuse, not a reason, for asking you to marry me. I'd been missing you for a long time and I came to Welford specifically to find you again and see if we couldn't get back together.'

'How very touching,' Norrie said sarcastically. 'But I couldn't care less what your motives were. I told you before that you leave me cold, but you're so damn big-headed that you just couldn't believe that a woman could find you repulsive.'

His face paled. 'Repulsive?'

'Yes, repulsive,' Norrie spat the word at him venomously. 'Did you seriously believe that I'd go to bed with a man who drove my father to his death?'

Bruno slowly dropped his hands, staring into her face. 'Christ, is that what this is all about, some kind of punishment for that?'

'Yes, that's exactly what it's about,' she flung at him. 'You were stupid enough to want to marry me, so I decided to show you just what the *institution* of marriage could mean.'

His mouth set into a grim line. 'And the way you've been acting tonight, all the teasing, it was just to turn the knife in the wound, was it?'

'Well, it did, didn't it? You were slobbering, you were so damn randy,' she retorted, hiding a sudden feeling of revulsion at her own behaviour.

Bruno's arm shot out and grabbed her. His mouth was twisted and his eyes dark with pain and anger. 'Shut up! You bitch, you sadistic little bitch. God help me, I've a good mind to . . .'

'To what?' Norrie demanded, her voice rising. 'To take me anyway? Just try it and I'll scream the place down. And try explaining to the management that your wife found you so abhorrent that you had to resort to rape on your wedding night.'

'But maybe it might not come to rape,' Bruno snarled, pushing her suddenly backwards so that she came up against the bed and fell on to it. Then he knelt over her, his legs on either side of hers, his weight holding her down. 'You aren't so immune to me. The way you've responded these last few weeks has proved that. You haven't even tried to resist when I've touched you.' And he deliberately put his hand on her breast, caressing her through the thin silk of the nightdress.

'Take your filthy hands off me,' she spat at him.

'Why don't you say what you really want?' he said roughly, jerking the strap off her shoulder and pulling it down, then cupping his hand round the soft swell of her bare skin.

'Now I'll have to scrub myself clean again, the same way I have every time after you've handled me.'

His face darkened and for a moment his hand tightened, hurting her. She tried not to wince but it must have shown on her face because he gave an ugly kind of smile. 'Why let me touch you then, if you find it so distasteful?'

'Just to keep you panting and eager, until tonight. You see I knew that sex and money were the only things you'd ever respond to.'

He stood up suddenly and turned his back on her. 'So why did you marry me?' he demanded harshly.

'For money, of course. What else?' Norrie stood up and replaced the strap of her nightdress; her breast felt sore even against the softness of the silk.

'And just what makes you think you're going to get any money out of me after this?' There was disgust in Bruno's face as he turned towards her.

'Oh, I think you'll be quite willing to pay up when you think of what will happen if you don't. Just think of the headlines: "Newspaper owner's wife sues for non-consummation".' She laughed sardonically. 'That won't do your precious image any good, will it? You'll be the laughing stock of everyone who knows you.'

'You can hardly sue for non-consummation when we have a son,' Bruno pointed out acidly.

'But you'd have to prove he was yours,' she said sweetly.

'You'd deny it?' he exclaimed.

'Of course.'

'Such things can be proved now, beyond doubt.'

'Sure. But you'd have to do it amid a blaze of dirty publicity from the gutter end of the national press. Is that what you want—for you or Ben?'

His jaw tightened. 'You're a lousy little blackmailer, Norrie. You'd even drag your own kid into this?'

'It can be avoided, if you pay.'

'How much?' he asked, his nostrils flaring disdainfully as if he had smelt something foul.

'Twenty thousand pounds,' she told him, waiting until she saw his quickly hidden surprise at the reasonableness of the demand before adding, 'for each of the people you kicked off the *Westland Gazette*—the ones that are still alive, that is.'

His eyes rested on her face in startled surprise. 'And for you?'

'Oh, I don't want anything from you. I'm just going to enjoy watching you squirm while you write out the cheques. Eight of them, making one hundred and sixty thousand pounds in all.' She said the amount slowly, emphasising the words.

'I can't lay my hands on that kind of money.'

'You can get it,' she said shortly. 'I don't expect you to write the cheques tonight. I'll give you time; I'll give you a whole month of time.'

'And what then?'

'Then we part and you can sue me for divorce.'

Bruno looked at her for a long moment, then, 'If I agree to your—proposition, then I'll want to legally adopt Ben.'

'No way.' Norrie's answer was swift and final.

'I married you to have a share in Ben's life.'

'Well, that's another price you'll have to pay. I've told you all along that Ben is nothing to do with you.'

'I'm not going to let you push me out of his life, Norrie. Not now.'

'You don't have a choice. Do you really think I'd let Ben grow up anywhere near someone as cruel as you?'

He glared at her morosely. 'I'm beginning to think I could take a few lessons in cruelty from you. How much will you take to give Ben up to me?'

Norrie stared at him. 'There isn't that much money in the world. Just get the hundred and sixty thousand for the people whose lives you ruined. And get it within a month.'

'That kind of money can't be raised that easily.'

'But you'd better. My father had friends who are pretty high up in Fleet Street; they'd willingly drag your name through the dirt if I asked them.'

'And your name, too,' he pointed out angrily.

'No, not my name, yours. I'm Mrs Denton now, remember?'

Bruno's face darkened and he took a menacing step towards her, reaching out to grab her wrist. But Norrie stepped swiftly backwards, moving her arm out of his reach. 'Don't you dare touch me,' she spat at him, revulsion in her face.

He recoiled as if she'd struck him, his hands balling into tight fists at his sides, and she suddenly realised what an effort it was costing him not to physically lash out at her. Well, so much the better. At least now he would learn what it was like to be hurt and just have to stand there and take it, just like her father and the other people on the *Westland Gazette* had had to take it from him.

Turning away, Bruno walked over to the dressing-table and picked up one of Ben's toys, a green hippopotamus, that he'd left there. 'It may take me longer than a month to raise that much money.'

'You know the consequences if you don't. And you're a very persuasive man; I'm sure you'll manage somehow.'

'And what reason do I give to the finance company or bank for that high a loan?'

'Well, you could always tell them that you're repaying an old debt.'

Lifting his head, he looked at her in the wide mirror above the dressing-table. 'Or that my wife is blackmailing me,' he said bitterly.

'Even that. I don't care if you mortgage the rest of your life away. Just get the money. However much you get wouldn't be enough to pay those people back.'

'This could ruin me.'

'So who cares?' she answered insolently. 'Did you care about them?'

'You're obsessed,' Bruno said angrily, his eyes fixed on her reflection. 'You've let this get to you so much that you can't even think straight any more. Let me make an appointment with someone you can talk it over with. Maybe that way you can . . .'

'A psychiatrist?' Norrie laughed disbelievingly. 'You're the one who's crazy—power crazy. Megalomania they call it, don't they? And that's why you wanted Ben, so that you would have someone else you could manipulate. I bet you . . .'

Her words were bitten off as Bruno suddenly dropped the toy and grabbed her arm, pulling her towards him. 'You said you didn't want anything from me,' he shouted savagely. 'But I gave you that nightdress, didn't I? So you won't want that!' And he began to drag at the straps, pulling it down to her waist and trying to tear it off.

Norrie opened her mouth and screamed.

For a few seconds Bruno went on tearing at the silk and it slid down to her hips, but then he brought up his hand to cover her mouth, the sudden silence more shattering than her scream. For a long moment their eyes clashed, both of them startled by the violence of their emotions, then the anger left them and Bruno's eyes grew bleak. Pushing her away, he turned and strode out of the bedroom, slamming the door behind him.

It was a few minutes before Norrie could move, but then she ran over to the door and locked it behind him. Her hands trembling almost uncontrollably, she took off the ruins of her nightdress and put on one of her own, then crawled into bed but left on the bedside light. Whether anyone had heard her scream or not she didn't know, but she was quite certain that Bruno had been goaded so far that, if she hadn't screamed, he would have taken her by force. She lay in bed wide awake, much too afraid to sleep, her heart still trembling even though he had walked away and the door was locked. Only after a long time did it occur to her that she had actually carried it through, that Bruno had had to accept her terms to repay the people he had harmed. That thought should have given her a big enough thrill to make everything worthwhile, but somehow it didn't. Where she should have been exultant at her success Norrie felt completely flat and empty. She kept remembering the way Bruno had looked when he said he had always loved her and the hurt and bitterness that replaced it when she told him she only wanted his money. That should have pleased her too, because they were the same emotions that she had been feeling for a very long time, but whoever said that revenge was sweet must have been lying, because Norrie felt almost as wretched now as she had the last time she'd rejected him.

CHAPTER SEVEN

NORRIE was awakened by a persistent knocking at the door. She came slowly out of a deep sleep, but then memory came flooding back and she immediately sat up, clutching the covers. Then she relaxed again, recognising the knock, and picked up the bedside clock. Eight o'clock, she could only have had about four hours' sleep. 'Okay, I'm coming,' she called, and got out of bed to unlock the door.

Ben was on the other side, wearing his new Action Man pyjamas and clutching a toy car that Bruno had given him. He came in and looked at the bed. 'Where that new Daddy gone?' he demanded.

Norrie got back into bed and he climbed in with her. 'Isn't he in your room, in the other bed? And what happened to my good-morning kiss?'

Putting his arms round her neck, Ben plonked a wet kiss on her cheek. 'Why that new Daddy not in this bed? He said . . .'

'I know, I know. But he isn't a real Daddy, pet. He's only a pretend Daddy.'

Ben was quite happy with that explanation; his world was full of pretend characters from books and the television. 'Has he gone away?'

'I'm not sure,' Norrie admitted cautiously. 'We'll have to wait and see.' She obligingly lifted her knees to make hills for him to run his car up and down, but he soon tired of this and she helped him wash and dress, then did so herself. After that, she wasn't quite sure whether to go down to breakfast or not, and had a sudden fear that Bruno might have walked out and left her to pay the hotel bill. But most of his clothes were still in the wardrobe in the bedroom, many of them with very good labels, she could always sell those to pay the bill and she had been careful to bring enough money to pay for her and Ben's return fare to Welford.

The breakfast room was already crowded, mostly with families making plans for the day. The sun was shining and the children were noisy, enjoying the added freedom they got from their parents' more relaxed, holiday mood. Norrie looked round for an empty table and saw Bruno sitting alone by a window, looking out at the view. Ben saw him, too, and tugged at her hand. 'There that new Daddy,' he exclaimed, loud enough for several tables to hear.

Her face flushed, Norrie let him lead her over to Bruno, out of embarrassment as much as anything else. Now all the hotel would think that she was having a clandestine holiday with him. Although, she thought with a grim, inward smile, nothing could be further from the truth.

Bruno stood up politely as they neared him, but his face was like a cold mask, completely and carefully devoid of any expression as he glanced at her. He pulled out a chair for her but then went to sit on the other side of the table, but he couldn't help smiling a little when Ben insisted on sitting next to him. 'Where you go?' he demanded.

'I went for a walk along the beach.'

Ben was indignant. 'Why you not take me? I like going for a walk on the beach.'

Bruno put a hand on the child's shoulder in a gesture that was both affectionate and reassuring. 'You were fast asleep, old chap.'

'Can we go down to the beach after breakfast?'

'That depends on your mother.' Bruno looked at Norrie fully for the first time, his eyes freezing her.

Ben frowned, not used to having Norrie referred to as his mother, 'That not my mother, that Norrie,' he pointed out to set the record straight.

But Bruno didn't hear him because Norrie spoke at the same time. 'It's your decision when we go back to London. After all,' she pointed out, 'I'm sure that you'd like to start on that—business you have to transact as soon as possible.'

Bruno's hand tightened on the handle of the coffee cup he was holding until the knuckles showed white, but his face gave nothing away. 'If you mean try to raise the money you're extorting out of me, I can't do much on a Sunday, so we might as well go down to the beach.'

The waiter came then and Ben kept up an excited stream of questions and remarks so that they both talked to him, which disguised the fact that they didn't talk to each other. After breakfast, they all went back to the suite to get ready for the beach, Bruno collecting some clothes and disappearing into the bathroom, while Norrie prudently changed into bikini and sundress in Ben's room.

The hotel had its own private stretch of beach reached from a path that twisted amid flowering shrubs down a low cliff. Ben tried to run ahead of them down the path, and Norrie called sharply, 'Ben, wait.' She tried to grab him but was too loaded up with bag and beach towels and Ben chortled happily as he ran away from her. In two strides Bruno caught him up and swung him up on to his shoulders, Ben not knowing whether to be angry at having his run for freedom curtailed or pleased to be up so high where he could see over the shrubs to the sea.

They found a vacant area near some rock pools, hired loungers and settled themselves down. It was a hot and lovely day, one of the few perfect days in an English summer, and already the people on the beach were in their swimming things, soaking up the sun while they got the chance. Ben wanted to make a sandcastle, so Bruno knelt in the sand to help him. While his back was turned, Norrie took off her sundress and began to apply suntan oil to her front. She had almost finished and was doing her arms when Bruno turned to get something and caught sight of her. His eyes darkened as they went over her tall, slender body, glistening gold in the sun, and Norrie felt as if she was standing there on the beach stark naked, her private femaleness exposed to his gaze. Instinctively she moved her hands to cover herself until she realised what she was doing. 'You louse!' she swore at him.

Bruno gave a small, sardonic smile and turned back to Ben.

Angrily Norrie stretched herself on the lounger, put on her sunglasses and picked up a book. For that, he could just look after Ben for the whole day for all she cared.

The sun was hot and Norrie was tired; soon she put the book down and closed her eyes, dozing. 'I'm taking Ben down to the sea for a swim,' Bruno's voice above her wakened her about half an hour later. He was standing over her, dressed in a pair of brief white bathing trunks, long legs slightly apart, his hands on his hips. He had a beautiful body, with muscles in all the right places, and Norrie's breath caught in her throat as she remembered that once they'd had a shower together and she had washed him all over before he hadn't been able to stand it any longer and had lifted her and then . . .

'Touché.' The irony in Bruno's voice brought her eyes flying up to his and she flushed, realising that she'd been staring.

'Ben can't swim,' she said, trying to get back to the commonplace.'

'So I'll teach him.'

'You be careful with him.' She sat up. 'He's all I've got.'

Bruno's eyes flashed with anger. 'Don't worry. He's all I've got, too,' he told her grimly.

Norrie watched them go down to the sea hand in hand, the tall man and the very small boy, her thoughts a mess. She had to fight a sudden, idiotic wish that the picture they represented was a true one; a man, a woman and their child. But it was all so much of a sham. More even than Bruno knew. She should have told him everything last night; she'd intended to at first, but he'd been so angry that she hadn't dared. Ben, she knew, was the main reason why he'd held his temper in check rather than the fear of her threats. He had enough strength to have silenced her screams and taken her if he'd really wanted to. But he hadn't because he was afraid of frightening his son, but if he'd known that Ben wasn't his ... They'd reached the sea now and Bruno was giving Ben his first swimming lesson, the water only coming up to his knees before it was deep enough for the child. Picking up her book, Norrie tried to read again but found it impossible to concentrate, and so sat watching them, thinking, remembering, wishing.

'Cigarette?'

Her thoughts were interrupted some time later and she blinked herself back to reality to find that a man who'd been sitting a few yards away had got up and was holding out a pack of cigarettes. He'd had a

woman and two young children with him, but Norrie
saw that they were down on the edge of the water. She
shook her head. 'No thanks, I don't.'

'No vices, eh?' The man gave an insincere laugh.
'Mind if I do?' He lit the cigarette and said, 'It's my
wife's turn to be at the kids' beck and call today. We
take it turn and turn about. Is that what you and your
husband do?'

'This is our first day here,' Norrie looked away,
hoping he would get the message, but the man
squatted down beside her on Bruno's lounger, told her
that he had already been there a week and proceeded
to advise her on where to go, the best times to eat in
the hotel, the best garage in the area, and a dozen
other things that Norrie hadn't remotely considered
she might want to know. He was a limpet, impossible
to get rid of without being downright rude, but Norrie
tried because she didn't like the way he kept eyeing
her or the familiar way he assumed that she wanted to
know him. Unfortunately he was still there when
Bruno brought Ben up from the beach. He stood up
and put out a hand to shake Bruno's. 'Hallo there. I'm
Tony Hills. Just been giving your wife a few pointers
about the hotel and that.'

Bruno didn't seem to see his hand; he nodded curtly
and looked at Norrie. 'Ben's thirsty. If you'll put some
dry trunks on him, I'll take him to get a drink.' The
other man cleared his throat, but when Bruno took no
further notice of him went back to his own patch of
beach where he was almost immediately joined by his
wife and children, the wife giving Norrie a somewhat
harassed and uncertain smile. As soon as he was out of
hearing, Bruno said derisively, 'You certainly don't
waste any time.'

'He spoke to me, and I couldn't get rid of him.'

Wrapping Ben in a towel, she pulled off his wet trunks and began to rub him dry.

'Really? I can't imagine any man staying near you unless you gave him come on signals.'

'Why not? You hung around and you certainly didn't get any come on signals when you came to Welford.' She helped Ben into his dry trunks. 'Come on, pet, put your shirt on now. It's getting hot and you don't want to get burnt.'

'No. Don't want it on.' Ben tried to pull away from her, throwing himself about as only a small, determined boy can.

'Put your shirt on. Do as Norrie tells you.'

Bruno's tone stopped Ben and he stood docilely as Norrie put on his shirt, but the fact that he'd obeyed Bruno somewhat annoyed her. She looked up at Bruno and said nastily, 'My, what a big he-man you are to little boys of three.'

Bruno's mouth tightened. 'Don't push it,' he warned.

But Norrie knew she was safe on the beach and chose to goad him. 'I shall do and say anything I damn well like, and until you pay the price you'll just have to put up with it, won't you?'

Anger flashed in his eyes and he opened his mouth to make a biting retort, but just then Ben gave a shout, and he turned to grab him down from where he'd already climbed about four feet up the cliff. 'Do you want a drink?' Bruno demanded with Ben under his arm.

'No.'

'Suit yourself.'

He strode off and didn't remember to put Ben down until the child beat at him with his fists.

Norrie turned over on her front and closed her

eyes, determined not to give the nearby family a chance to speak to her again. She must have dozed off again because the next thing she felt was a rush of cold water on her back. 'Hey! Stop.' She sat up to find Ben grinning at her warily, an empty plastic bucket in his hands. 'Why you little monkey.' Norrie jumped up and he gave a shriek of fear and excitement and fled to a safe distance before he stopped to make sure that she wasn't chasing him. 'Ugh, it was half full of sand and pebbles.' She tried to wipe some off her back and then saw the grin on Bruno's face. 'I suppose you put him up to that. It's the sort of small-minded thing you would do.'

Bruno's face changed and he reached out and took hold of her wrist, hurting her. 'Don't you dare accuse *me* of being small-minded.'

'Let go of me, you're hurting.'

'Too bad.' He grinned insolently down at her.

'I say—er—is anything wrong?' It was the other man from the hotel.

Bruno glanced at him and said maliciously, 'Not a thing. Is there, darling?' And jerking her forward, he put his arm round her and kissed her.

'You pig!' Norrie moved away as soon as he released her and lifted her hand to wipe her mouth, glaring at him. Then, her hair swirling like a golden flame about her head, she turned and ran after Ben, chasing him through the soft sand.

They spent the rest of the day on the beach except for a break at lunchtime, but Norrie was far from enjoying it. She didn't like the way the man sitting nearby kept looking at her or the admiring glances his wife kept giving Bruno whenever she thought Norrie wasn't looking. And it didn't help when Ben started playing with their children so that Norrie had to answer when they spoke to her, out of common politeness. Bruno just lay back on his lounger, closed his eyes and appeared to go to sleep, but whether he really was or not was debatable because Norrie could have sworn that he once or twice snorted derisively when Tony Hills paid her a compliment.

It was almost a relief when it was time to go back to the hotel for the evening, and because Ben ate separately, they were able to more or less avoid one another until it was time for dinner. Bruno had gone down ahead to the bar and Norrie reluctantly joined him, making sure that she was wearing one of her own dresses. And she was glad she had, because it was soon pretty obvious that he had already had several drinks. Not that his speech was at all slurred or anything, and no one looking at him could possibly tell, but his anger was more brittle and his emotions weren't so successfully hidden or held in check. He had another double Scotch before they went in for their meal, and he drank nearly a bottle and a half of wine during it. Then he had brandy afterwards although Norrie refused. She was treading very warily, not speaking unless he spoke to her and then being terribly careful in what she said. The last thing she wanted was a scene in the dining-room, or to provoke him into anything drastic when they got to their suite and shut out the rest of the hotel. He had a brooding look she didn't like and Norrie decided to stay down in the lounge for as long as possible.

So when Tony Hills and his wife came up to join them, Norrie smiled and made them welcome, encouraging them to talk and stay there. But their company also had an adverse effect because Tony ordered another round of drinks and after that the men took it in turns.

It was a hellish couple of hours; Tony tried to flirt covertly with Norrie and his wife was ogling Bruno, who kept laughing when he shouldn't and not when Tony told one of his rather risqué jokes. And it was all a mistake because Bruno was drinking more than he would have done if they'd been by themselves.

At length, getting desperate, Norrie stood up and said, 'If you'll excuse me, I'm going to bed. All this fresh air has made me tired.'

'What a good idea.' Bruno caught her arm, 'I'll come with you.'

'Oh, that's all right, you stay and chat. I don't mind going up alone.'

'Oh, but I wouldn't dream of it.' He finished his drink and stood up, his fingers biting into her arm. 'Good night.' He nodded to the others.

'Er—before you go, old chap, I wonder if I might have a word,' Tony said, also getting to his feet.

'Yes?' Bruno raised his eyebrows.

'In—er—private, if I might, old man.'

Bruno frowned, but said, 'Oh, very well.' And the two men went off.

Norrie groaned inwardly as she escaped upstairs. Oh, hell, I bet he's going to ask Bruno to lend him some money. That will just about push him over the edge. Going into the suite, she hurriedly made sure that Ben was okay and then went into the bedroom, only to stand transfixed when she saw that the key wasn't in the lock. She yanked the door open again but the key wasn't in the other side. Bruno must have removed it earlier and she hadn't noticed. She waited for him to come upstairs, furious enough now not to be afraid.

She stood in the middle of the sitting-room, ready to let fly at him, but when Bruno walked into the room the words died in her throat as she saw his face. He was laughing, but it was an angry, sardonic kind of laugh that appalled her. 'What is it? What did he want?'

'What did he want, your friend Tony Hills?' Bruno leant back against the wall and shook with laughter, then he straightened up and came over to her, put a hand on her neck and caressed her cheek with his thumb, not roughly, but not gently either. 'I'll tell you what he wanted, my lovely bride.' For a moment his hand tightened. 'Your—filthy little admirer wanted to do a swap tonight, his wife for mine.'

'He what?' Norrie stared at him in horror.

'Mm. Ironical, isn't it, when you think about it? He casually asked for what I haven't even had myself.' And he began to laugh again.

'How dare he? The vile, horrible . . . What did you say?' She caught hold of his lapels. 'Bruno, what did you say to him?'

'What? Oh, I didn't say anything. I just hit him.' He grinned. 'And I damn well enjoyed it, too,' he added, flexing his knuckles in remembrance.

'Good. I'm glad. I hope you knocked him down. As if I'd even contemplate going to bed with a creep like him. Surely they could see that when I was with you I wouldn't want anyone else?'

Bruno laughed. 'Yes, I did knock him down. He's probably still lying out there in the garden.' Then he seemed to realise what she'd said, because he stopped laughing. 'Wouldn't you want anyone else?'

Her anger evaporated as she looked into his eyes. 'No,' she admitted after a long moment.

Lifting his hand, he placed it on the other side of her face and stared down into her eyes. 'What the hell happened to us, Norrie?'

She tried to shake her head but couldn't. 'I don't know,' she admitted wretchedly.

'Couldn't we start over again, couldn't we?' he asked earnestly, a note almost of pleading in his voice.

For a moment Norrie closed her eyes tightly, then said, 'No. It's too late.'

'Not if we try. Surely we can try. For Ben's sake if nothing else.'

Tears gathered in her eyes. 'Bruno, Ben isn't . . .'

But he bent and kissed her, his lips compulsively taking hers, desperately seeking and slowly getting a response. He held her head in his hands and kissed her for a long time, only reluctantly lifting his head to look down at her closed eyes and sensuously parted lips. Slowly Norrie came back to reality and read the unspoken question in his eyes. It would be so easy to just nod and let him pick her up and carry her into the bedroom, to close the door and . . . Her eyes suddenly opened wide and she stepped away from him. 'What's this—plan B? Or just something you cooked up on the spur of the moment?' she demanded fiercely.

Bruno's eyebrows went up in surprise. 'I don't know what you mean.'

'No? Well, you must certainly know what plan A is.'

'What plan? What are you talking about?'

'Your plan to get me into bed with you,' Norrie answered contemptuously. 'Were you going to try charm again or just force your way in? Why else would you take the key out of my bedroom door?'

He shoved his hands in his pockets. 'I haven't got the damn key.'

'Who else would take it? Give it to me.'

'I haven't got it I tell you.'

'Don't lie, Bruno. You had it all worked out earlier

today that you'd . . .'

'Well, you're damn well wrong. And you don't need the key because you're safe enough from me. I'm not going to try and force myself on you when Ben's in the next room. If you don't know that you ought to.' Striding past her, he pushed open the bedroom door and looked at the lock and then inside the room. 'Come here.' He was pointing inside and when Norrie went up to him she saw the key lying on the carpet a few feet away. 'It must have fallen out. Ben swung the door pretty hard when he was anxious to get down to the beach this morning, didn't he?'

'Yes.' Norrie bent to pick up the key. 'I—I'm sorry.'

Bruno looked at her, his mouth set into a thin line. 'We'll leave here in the morning,' he said shortly.

The London flat was large but had only two bedrooms, one of which contained a kingsize double bed, and the other Bruno had had redecorated to suit a three year old boy, with wallpaper depicting colourful trains, boats and planes, and red and white miniature-sized furniture. With his expected new way of life in ruins, Bruno ended up in the child's room and Norrie and Ben shared the big bed for a couple of nights until she bought a put-u-up for the boy which she squeezed into a corner of the larger bedroom.

She had thought that once they were in London and Bruno going to his office every day, the atmosphere between them would clear a little, but somehow the tension became daily worse and it was only Ben's presence that many times stopped it from exploding. It came very near to it once when Norrie bought Ben some new clothes which he insisted on wearing, running to meet Bruno at the door when he came in shouting, 'Look at my new trousers. I've got four pockets.'

'Hey, that's more than I've got.' Bruno put down his briefcase and picked him up to have a closer look.

'And I've got a new shirt and some new shoes. Look.'

Bruno dutifully admired everything and carried Ben into the kitchen where Norrie was cooking dinner, but Ben immediately demanded to be set down so that he could go back and watch the television. 'It smells good,' Bruno remarked, but Norrie didn't turn round. 'What is it?'

'Beef in a pastry case.'

'Sounds delicious.' He reached into his hip pocket for his wallet. 'I went to the bank today.'

Norrie turned swiftly at that. 'They've agreed to lend you the money?'

His mouth grew grim. 'I merely drew out some cash. You'll need some more housekeeping money.'

'No.' Norrie turned back to the ceramic hob to continue stirring the gravy. 'I have plenty left from the money you gave me on Monday.'

'But you bought clothes for Ben today.'

'Yes, *I* bought them. With my own money, not out of what you provided. I only use that for your share of the food.'

Bruno gripped her arm and pulled her round to face him so that the spoon fell out of her hand and spilt gravy on the marbled work surface. 'Just how much of that money I gave you have you used?'

'It's in the top drawer over there,' she answered defensively.

Jerking open the drawer, he put in his hand and quickly counted through the small pile of notes. 'You've hardly touched this money.'

'Yes, I have. I told you: I used it to buy your share of the food.'

Anger darkened his eyes. 'And you've paid for the rest out of your own money, I suppose.'

'Yes, of course. Because . . .'

'Because you don't want anything from me,' Bruno finished for her. 'Yes, I remember you telling me that. But Ben is my son and if he needs anything I'll provide it. And as for you,' his eyes dwelt on her scornfully, 'while you're under my roof then you're my guest. And I don't expect my guests to pay for their own food.'

'You can hardly call me a guest,' Norrie retorted, remembering how she had scrupulously divided everything she'd spent on food. 'And I should have thought you'd need every penny you can get towards paying off your debts. Have you raised the money yet?'

'Mind your own damn business,' Bruno flashed harshly.

'It is my business. The sooner you raise it the sooner I can leave. You don't think I enjoy being here, do you?'

'How and when I get the money is my affair, and you'll just have to wait to find out when you can put your stupidly misguided philanthropy into practice,' he told her with a sneer.

Norrie's temper blew. 'It isn't philanthropy; they're debts you owe only you won't admit it. And I'm not going to use your money. I don't want to be kept by you for even a minute.'

Bruno laughed unpleasantly. 'Afraid of being thought a kept woman? You needn't worry; you're not the type any man would choose for a mistress.'

'Why you . . .' Picking up an empty bowl, Norrie

threw it at his head, but he ducked and it shattered
against the wall. The next second he'd grabbed her
and they were fighting in the small confines of the
kitchen, Norrie trying to tear at him with her nails and
Bruno easily holding her off. So she kicked him on the
shin, hard.

'Ouch! You bitch.' Bruno tried to catch her wrist
and a cup went flying from the table to smash on the
tiled floor.

They were so intent on fighting one another that
neither of them noticed Ben come into the room. He
threw himself at Bruno, grabbing one of his legs and
holding on to it with both arms and legs, then tried to
bite Bruno through his trousers.

'Hey.' Bruno reached down and had to tug hard to
pull him off.

'Don't hurt Norrie! Don't hurt Norrie!' Tears were
streaming down Ben's face and he was hitting out at
Bruno with his small fists.

'Oh hell!' Bruno exclaimed with real pain in his
face. 'It's all right. Norrie and I were only playing.
Like you and I pretend to fight. We pretend, don't
we?' He held Ben close and kissed his wet cheeks. 'It's
all right, old son. Don't cry.'

But Ben pushed away from him and held his arms
out to Norrie. She took him and sat down in a chair,
cuddling him to her, letting him feel the security of
her warmth and closeness, her head close to his.

Bruno watched them for a moment, then said
abruptly, 'I'm going out.'

Norrie raised her head, feeling suddenly deathly
tired and sad. 'What about dinner?' she asked
mechanically.

'To hell with it.' And he strode out of the flat.

After that they were both very careful to control

their feelings, speaking to each other with icy politeness when Ben was around, and trying to ignore one another when he wasn't. But emotions held in check only served to increase the tension. Norrie felt as if her nerves were taut wires that could snap at any second. The days, when Bruno was at work, weren't too bad, she could take Ben out to see the sights of London or walk with him in Regent's Park, but as the day wore on and she knew that the time for seeing Bruno was coming closer, she grew more and more uptight.

The evenings, after Ben had gone to bed, were the worst; she dreaded the long summer nights when she had hung out clearing up the kitchen for as long as possible and would have to join Bruno in the sitting-room, the two of them in the same room together and yet a million miles apart. Mostly she read, because that gave her a barrier of preoccupation that he couldn't easily break through, but it was almost impossible to concentrate when Bruno sat broodingly in his armchair, his eyes more often on her than on the television set, the tension between them mounting to screaming point as the days went by.

Ben was a very lively boy and, like every other child in the world, never wanted to go to bed, especially on the light summer evenings, so it was easy to give in to him and let him stay up to watch the end of his television programme, to take longer over giving him his bath, and to read him the extra bedtime story that he always demanded.

Norrie knew that she was over-indulging him and began to feel desperately guilty when it got to nearly nine before he finally went to sleep, but it was only for a short time and often she would carry on reading aloud after he'd gone to sleep because that way there was only an hour or so of the evening left to get through with Bruno before she could retreat to bed herself. When she had gone into this it had been on a wave of anger that had carried her along, and it had all seemed so simple; to make Bruno pay and then go back to her old life. But the stark reality of having to live with him in this electric tension while he raised the money was almost more than she could bear, so Norrie gradually let the boy stay up later and later until he grew fretful and almost asleep on his feet. Bruno watched grimly, knowing exactly what she was doing, and it led, inevitably, to the clash that she had been trying to avoid.

It was gone ten one night when Norrie finally came out of Ben's room; he was fast asleep and she couldn't pretend any longer to be reading him a story, but it was late enough now for her to go to bed herself. Bruno was sitting in an armchair with a drink in his hand, watching television, but his eyes followed her as she went into the kitchen to wash up Ben's supper dishes. She poured a glass of milk and put a couple of biscuits on a plate for her own supper, thinking that she could eat them in bed and read a book until she felt tired enough to go to sleep.

The kitchen door opened behind her and Bruno came in. 'I want to talk to you,' he said coldly.

'But I don't particularly want to talk to you,' Norrie retorted, picking up the plate and glass. 'Unless of course you're going to tell me that you've raised the money at last.'

'At last?'

'It's getting very boring being stuck here in the flat with you every evening,' she told him baldly.

'Which is why you spend as much time as possible in the kitchen and let Ben stay up so late, I suppose?'

'Of course. Anyone's company is better than yours.'

'You're taking this out on the child. He's tired out and nothing like the lively boy he was before you came here.'

'Before he had to live with you, you mean. If you want him to be happy again, you'll hurry up and let me go home.'

'No one's stopping you,' Bruno pointed out icily.

'Oh no, I'm not leaving here until you pay what you owe—or until I tell my story to the press. And until then I shall avoid you as much as possible.'

'You didn't used to object to my company once,' he reminded her acidly.

'That was a long time ago, before I realised what you were really like. A lifetime ago.'

'Ben's lifetime ago,' he said forcefully. 'Don't take your frustration out on him, Norrie.' The words were a command not a plea.

'Frustration?' She gave a high, slightly hysterical laugh and put down the things she was holding. 'Oh, that's funny, it really is. Can't you ever think about anything but sex? I'm not in the least frustrated. I told you before that you don't turn me on any more. Quite the reverse. You just make me feel—unclean.'

Bruno's jaw tightened in anger. 'Really?' he taunted. 'That wasn't the way I read it. The way you responded during our so-called engagement made it pretty obvious that you were sex-starved.'

'I was what?' Norrie demanded incredulously, her voice rising. 'My God, do you think that you're the only man I've ever had? Well, you're not, not by a long chalk. I've had plenty of boyfriends since you. And they were all better in bed than you ever were.'

Unable to keep his hands off her any longer, Bruno reached out and caught her wrist. 'That's a very sweeping statement,' he said with biting anger. 'And if it's true, you'll have learnt a whole load of new tricks. Why don't you tell me about them; maybe I'll learn something. That would make a change, wouldn't it? You teaching me.' He pulled her close to him and held her arms behind her back. 'Well, go on. I'm waiting to hear. Tell me all these things your dozens of lovers have taught you—or is it hundreds?' he added savagely.

'Let go of me or I'll scream.'

'And wake Ben? Yes, that's the sort of thing you would do. Playing on a child's happiness to grab what you want. How the hell do you think he feels about all this?'

'He's too young to understand. And it's only for two more weeks; if you haven't got the money by then I shall take him away.'

'And subject him to everything the gutter press can do. His photograph in the papers, pointed out in the street, his life made a misery.'

'No,' Norrie interrupted fiercely. 'I won't let Ben come into it. Those are the things that will happen to you, not him. You'll be the one who is pointed out and laughed at.'

He stared down at her. 'I believe you really do hate me.'

She laughed mirthlessly. 'I have cause enough.'

But he went on as if she hadn't spoken. 'But you want me, even so. Whatever you say, whatever your mind tells you, your body still wants to be loved. And that's what you hate more than anything else; the fact that your body betrays you every time. You want me, Norrie, admit it.'

'No, that isn't so.' She tried to break free of his hold, but when she did her body rubbed against his and he grinned.

'Perhaps you'd like me to make you admit it. I've a feeling I can, quite easily.' His eyes looked down into hers in mocking anger.

'Let go of me, Bruno. This isn't funny.'

'What's the matter, has the game got out of hand? Have I called your bluff?' Bending his head he began to kiss her neck. 'You like it when I kiss you" he murmured, his lips soft against her skin. 'Do you think I don't know? You drown in them. I can read it in your eyes. Feel it in your pulse. You don't want it, but you can't resist.' His mouth moved to the corner of hers, began to move along her lower lip with light kisses that were little more than a touch.

Norrie stood rigidly within his hold, determined not to yield an inch, to let him see by her complete indifference just how wrong he was. But then his tongue pushed insidiously between her lips, softly exploring the warmth of her mouth and she jerked her head back, her eyes spitting hate. 'Get away from me,' she yelled hysterically. 'Get away.'

He laughed, knowing he'd proved his point, and let her go contemptuously. 'Just promise not to take it out on Ben any more. Put him to bed at his normal time. If my being here bugs you that much we can take it in turns to go out in the evening.'

Norrie rubbed her wrist where he'd held her and glared at him. 'I hate you,' she said balefully. 'God, how I hate you.'

But he only laughed again and said, 'But now we both know why, don't we?'

She couldn't take any more, turning, Norrie ran out of the kitchen and into the bedroom with the sound of his mockery ringing in her ears.

Thinking about it, she knew that Bruno was right about Ben and the next day she put him to bed at seven. At eight Bruno went out and didn't come back until after she was in bed. He didn't say where he was going and she didn't ask. Their relationship was strained now, to say the least, and Norrie found it a relief to go out the following evening. She went to see a film in the West End, but it felt strange going to a cinema by herself, and she hadn't seen an adult film for ages. The only ones she'd seen were Walt Disney productions with Ben, who'd sat entranced the whole way through, holding tightly to Norrie's hand and burying his head in her lap whenever a wicked character came along, and shouting with the best of them when the cavalry—in whatever form it took— arrived in the nick of time. It felt almost sinful to sit back in the comfortable seat with a bar of her favourite chocolate. Norrie had no real worries about leaving Ben with Bruno, but somehow she just couldn't enjoy the film. She felt restless and strangely lonely, but sat there until the film ended, not really taking it in.

When she got back to the flat Bruno was still up, stretched out on the settee listening to Mozart from his quadrophonic speakers. He had a good collection of recordings and his equipment gave a first class reproduction. Norrie sat in the other chair and let the music engulf her, her eyes closed as she listened. When it finished, she opened them reluctantly and found that Bruno was watching her. 'Maybe we should listen to music more often,' he suggested lazily. 'We haven't taken a knife to each other for over half an hour.'

Norrie sat up to retaliate but saw that he wasn't trying to goad her and leaned back. 'Maybe we should,' she agreed. 'Was Ben okay?'

'Fine. Not a peep out of him. How was your film?'

'How do you know I went to a film?' she countered.

'I could have gone to a concert, or a play. Or to pick up a man,' she added provocatively.

But he didn't rise to the bait. 'You left the paper open at the entertainments page and you'd marked off the films with a pencil,' he told her with a grin.

'Oh. Well, it was okay, I suppose.'

'That doesn't sound as if you enjoyed it very much.'

'No, not much. I'm not used to going on my own,' she admitted without thinking.

'You mean you'd rather have been in the back row with one of your many lovers,' Bruno sneered.

Norrie didn't say anything, but just stood up and walked out of the room.

The next day was Friday with the long weekend when Bruno would be at home looming over her, but two things happened that day to take her mind off it, both of which gave her very mixed feelings. The first arrived in the way of a letter, forwarded to her from Welford. It was from her brother, Geoff, which was a surprise in itself, for he seldom wrote to her. The letter told her that he had met a French woman out in Saudi Arabia and was going to marry her fairly soon. 'So we have the problem of Ben,' the letter went on and Norrie's heart stood still at the thought of losing the child. 'Michelle is divorced and has two daughters of her own. She doesn't mind taking on Ben but is quite happy to leave him with you, if you will still have him. Quite frankly, I would rather you kept him. You know all the reasons why. And also, when I finish here in six months, I will be going to France with Michelle to live permanently. I have been offered a job there near Lyons.

'If you do decide to keep Ben, I think we should put it on a legal footing and I will let you legally adopt him. I will still continue to send the money for his keep, of course, so nothing will really change. Please let me know what you decide and, if yes, take this letter to my solicitor who will put all the legal arrangements in hand.'

It took a couple of readings before all the implications of the letter sank in. Ben would be really her own, forever. But he would have to grow up knowing that his own father had rejected him. And right now was the worst time to take up adoption proceedings in case Bruno found out. She would rather he went on thinking that Ben was his until after he'd paid up and she was safely away from him. But there was no question of her not wanting Ben, even if she was thought of as an unmarried mother for the rest of her life. She folded the letter carefully and zipped it into one of the compartments of her handbag; she must be careful not to let Bruno see it and to destroy it as soon as she'd been to Geoff's solicitor.

She 'phoned them and made an appointment for the following week and had hardly put the 'phone down before it rang again.

'Bruno, darling,' said a husky female voice before Norrie could speak. 'It's Katie. I'm here in London. I got back from America earlier this week, and you were the first man I thought of to spend the weekend with. Bruno?' the voice paused questioningly.

'I'm afraid this isn't Bruno,' Norrie said silkily, enjoying the moment. 'He isn't here.'

'Are you the domestic help?' the woman asked coldly.

'Not quite. As a matter of fact I'm his wife. You must have been away some time.'

'Not that long. But it was obviously long enough for

you to move in,' the woman said with a trace of bitterness.

'Well, don't let that stop you. If you'll give me your number I'll tell him to call you back.'

'You don't mind him going out with someone else so soon?' The voice sounded incredulous.

'Oh, we have a very open marriage,' Norrie replied airily. 'And I'm sure he could do with a little— diversion by now.'

The girl gave her number and the two receivers went down together. Norrie sat staring at the 'phone as if it could tell her what the other girl was like. She had certainly sounded extremely sexy and sophisticated, and Norrie felt a stab of something that was very close to jealousy. Well, she could probably have been sexy and sophisticated herself if she hadn't met Bruno, and hadn't had Ben to look after. But then she remembered the words Bruno had whispered on their farcical wedding night: that he'd never stopped loving her, had never wanted to marry anyone else. And he'd chosen her over his sexy-voiced girl-friend. Or was that all for Ben? To keep her happy as the mother of his son?

Dinner was waiting when Bruno came home at six that evening and when they'd eaten and Ben had run into the sitting-room to watch a cowboy film, Norrie said casually, 'There was a call for you today. Or at least it was for Bruno daahling,' she imitated the sexy tone. 'From somebody called Katie who had a voice like a deflating water bed and wanted to know if you were available for the weekend.'

Bruno lifted his head and looked at her steadily. 'And what did you say?'

'Oh, I told her I couldn't think of a thing to stop you,' Norrie answered off-handedly. 'Her number is on the pad by the 'phone. I should hurry,' she added tauntingly, 'she must be near the bottom of her list if she'd got to you.'

Beyond giving her an unpleasant look, Bruno said nothing further but went into the main bedroom to use the extension 'phone. Norrie would have given a lot to lift the one in the kitchen and listen but pride prevented her. When he came out of the bedroom half an hour later he had bathed and changed. 'See you later,' he said casually.

'Don't keep Katie daahling waiting,' Norrie taunted, hoping for information.

But Bruno merely smiled mockingly. 'I won't.'

And then he was gone and for some reason Norrie had to pick up a cushion and throw it at the closed door, 'Damn you, Bruno Denton! Damn you. Damn you. Damn you.'

CHAPTER EIGHT

BRUNO didn't come home until very late. Norrie had gone to bed a couple of hours earlier but couldn't sleep; she kept tossing and turning, wishing that it was all over and she and Ben were back home in their own little cottage. In the morning she woke feeling more tired than when she'd gone to bed, and found it difficult not to be ratty with Ben. But Bruno she could be as ratty with as she liked. She made breakfast for Ben and herself, but when Bruno came in ostentatiously picked up the morning paper, leaving him to get his own breakfast.

He did so without comment after looking at her set face, and devoted himself to talking to Ben. 'What would you like to do today?' he asked him.

'Go to the zoo,' Ben replied without hesitation; he loved the animals, especially the tigers, giving a shriek and running away whenever one of them roared.

'Okay, the zoo it is. And how about if we take a picnic and eat it in the park first?'

Ben clapped his hands. 'Yes, yes. I like picnics.' Then his face changed. 'Can Norrie come on the picnic, too?'

'Of course Norrie will come, too,' Bruno said firmly.

She deigned to lower her paper. 'Thanks for asking me,' she said sarcastically. 'Has it occurred to you that I might have other plans?'

'Have you?' he asked equably, pouring himself another cup of coffee.

'I might not want to go to the zoo,' she snapped, cornered.

'Why not, it's as good a place as any.'

'Possibly because I've already been there four times in the last two weeks.'

Bruno laughed. 'But Ben liked it so much when you took him that he wants to go again. Don't you, son?'

'Yes.' Ben looked at Norrie worriedly, not understanding what was going on. 'Please, Norrie.'

She looked at his pleading face and sighed. 'Okay, you win. But you've got to help get the picnic ready.'

'Yes.' He gave her a big hug and a wet kiss and went off to find his toy tiger to take with him.

When he'd gone Bruno looked at her disparagingly. 'You knew you'd come so why make all the fuss? It only confuses the child.'

'My,' Norrie pretended to look at him admiringly. 'For someone who's been a father for only a few weeks you've really become an expert,' she told him sarcastically.

'It doesn't take an expert to use common sense.' He stood up. 'Have we got food for a picnic?'

'It was your idea, you look,' she answered rudely.

'That's fine by me. Why don't you take that paper that you find so interesting and go into the other room while we get everything ready?'

So Norrie more or less had to sit by herself listening to Ben's excited laughter as he 'helped' Bruno. And Bruno, too, was laughing. They seemed to be having a great time in there, she thought viciously.

They walked across to the park and went up to where the Grand Union Canal wound its slow way through the green heart of London. Ben fed the swans and watched the gaily-painted narrow boats go through the lock before consenting to find a sheltered spot in the shade of an old, gnarled oak tree in which to have their picnic. Bruno had really gone to town; there was not only a well-filled hamper, but also a bottle of wine in a keep-cool pack, glasses, and even a tablecloth to lay it all out on.

'Nice,' Ben said, which was high praise for him and bit into the small rolls Bruno had cut specially for him. It was a far cry from the plastic airtight box of paste sandwiches and flask of orange squash that usually constituted their picnics back in Welford.

They ate well and finished with coffee. Ben, ever polite, said, 'Please may I leave the tablecloth,' and ran to play with his ball while they drank it, then came back and sat on Norrie's lap. The sun had gone round so that they were no longer in the shade, and she lay back on the grass, enjoying its warmth, with Ben lying in the crook of her arm, his head on her chest, taking his afternoon nap. She must have dozed herself but woke when Ben moved away and began to play with his ball again, kicking it backwards and forwards and then round and round the tree.

'There's more coffee, if you want some,' Bruno said as she sat up.

'No, thanks.' She got to her feet, rubbing her arm where Ben's weight had lain. 'I think I'll walk a little.'

To her surprise, Bruno got up to join her and they strolled a few yards down the path, always in sight and sound of Ben. 'You looked very—maternal with Ben sleeping there in your arms. I should imagine that you're a good mother to him when you're not in the grip of emotions you can't control.'

Norrie turned on him to retaliate. 'I'm *always* a good mother to him. And I'm always . . .' Her voice died away at the strange look she saw in his face. 'What is it?'

He hesitated and looked away, his hands thrust into the pockets of his tailored jeans. Then he stopped and turned to face her. 'I suppose I'd better tell you.' For a moment she thought that he was going to tell her about the other girl, that he wanted an annulment to marry her or something, and Norrie felt a stupid wave of relief when he said, 'It's about the money you want.'

'You've got it? I'm—I'm glad.' And she began to envisage everything that would mean.

Bruno straightened his shoulders as if about to take a blow. 'No, I haven't got it. I haven't even tried to get it.'

Norrie's eyes widened. 'What do you mean? Why not?'

'Because I've been hoping that you'd come to your senses and see just how stupid and unreasonable you're being.'

'You mean you're not going to pay those people?' Norrie exclaimed, her voice rising angrily.

'No, I'm not. You don't want to help them, you just want to hurt me.'

'You had no intention, then, of getting that money? You've just been—been stringing me along, right from the start.' Norrie was furiously angry now, glaring at him accusingly, unable to think about anything else.

'I've been hoping that you'd realise that what you're doing is just getting your own back on me for going against you all those years ago. You asked me not to sack your father but I went ahead and did it. And you just couldn't take that. You couldn't accept that I'd put anything ahead of my love for you.'

'Shut up!' Norrie shouted at him. 'You're just trying to make excuses in the hope that I'll let you off the hook. Well, I won't. You rotten swine! Why the hell didn't you tell me that you weren't going to pay up right from the start? I'll make you sorry for the weeks I've had to spend with you, you see if I don't.'

Raising her arm she took a swipe at him, but Bruno caught her wrist and glared down at her. 'You silly bitch,' he said harshly. 'Why won't you admit your own feelings? Why can't you just forget about the past and listen to . . .'

'Oh, that child!' A woman's high scream cut through his words and they both spun round, knowing instinctively that it was about Ben. They had completely forgotten about him during their quarrel.

For a moment Norrie couldn't see him, but then she followed the woman's pointing hand and saw Ben high up in the branches of the tree! He was clinging to a branch with one hand and reaching out for another, just like Tarzan, one of his favourite television characters. Just like Tarzan! Norrie began to run on legs that suddenly seemed like lead, and felt that she would never reach him. But Bruno was before her, rapidly covering the twenty or so yards between them and the tree. But even so he was too late. Ben missed the other branch and fell, plunging through the foliage like a broken bird and catching himself on the metal railings that surrounded the tree trunk before landing heavily on the ground.

'Ben!' Norrie screamed out his name and threw herself forward. 'Ben!' She reached to take his still body in her arms but Bruno held her off.

'Don't touch him.'

'No! Ben, Ben,' Norrie cried out in terror and tried to fight Bruno to let her hold him.

'He mustn't be moved! Go and get an ambulance.' But Norrie was screaming hysterically and he suddenly caught hold of her shoulder and slapped her face. She stared at him, glassy eyed, her breath hiccuping in her throat. 'Run to the zoo entrance and get an ambulance. Go on.'

She looked wildly down at Ben. 'He's bleeding.'

'I'll take care of it. Now run!'

With a sob, Norrie turned to obey him, running as she'd never run before, the quarter of a mile to the zoo entrance, there to incoherently cry out her plea to use their 'phone, to get an ambulance, her son was hurt. To hurry, hurry. And those wonderful men knew exactly what to do and made her stay until the ambulance came, only a couple of minutes later, and then climb in to show the driver the way.

She was out of the vehicle before it had stopped moving and pushed her way ruthlessly through the small crowd that had gathered. Ben was still lying on the ground, unconscious and deathly pale, but Bruno had tied a cloth round his torn leg, although this was already stained red. 'Oh God! Oh God!' The words were a terrified prayer as she went down on her knees beside the child, but the ambulance men were immediately behind her and gently moved her aside so that they could attend to him.

Bruno lifted her to her feet and held her, but she didn't even notice. Her eyes were fixed on Ben's face and her mind was filled with just one silent, frantic prayer. 'Don't die. Please don't die. Oh God, don't let him die.' Repeated over and over and over, her mind, her body, her very existence given over to that one distraught and frenzied plea.

'Are you the boy's parents?' The ambulance man stood up.

'Yes.' Bruno answered for them.

'Let's get him to hospital, then.' They gently lifted his small form on to a stretcher and covered it with a red blanket before putting him into the ambulance. Norrie and Bruno sat on the opposite side and watched as the ambulance attendant put an oxygen mask over Ben's face.

'How is he? Can you tell?' The words seemed torn from Bruno, as if he was afraid to ask.

'I don't think he's broken any limbs,' the man said and left them to worry about all the things he hadn't said.

The driver had radioed ahead to the hospital and he was whisked into Casualty so fast that they almost had to run to keep up. Then a woman stepped in front of them to hold them back as Ben was pushed through doors that took him beyond the reach of anything but their thoughts and prayers.

'If you could give me some information it would help a great deal,' the woman said smoothly, used to dealing with frantic relations and knowing exactly what to say and how to say it. 'Let's sit down so that I can write, shall we?'

She led the way to some chairs in the waiting area and Bruno pulled Norrie down into the seat beside him, but she immediately stood up again, her hands tightly clasped together, her eyes staring at the door they'd taken Ben through. 'Please, please, please.'

'I take it you're the boy's father?' And when Bruno nodded, 'Could I have the child's name and address please?'

Dimly she was aware of Bruno answering but didn't really listen until he pulled at her arm. 'They want Ben's blood group; do you know it?'

'No.' She shook her head wildly.

The clerk turned to Bruno again. 'Well, do you know your blood group? If we find out the parents', it helps.'

Bruno began to speak but Norrie said distractedly, 'His blood group won't be any use. He isn't Ben's father.'

There was a startled, shattering silence as the clerk looked at Bruno's stunned face, then she tactfully turned away and said to Norrie, 'Well, yours then?'

'He isn't mine,' she answered on a wild, terrified note. 'That is, he's mine, but I'm not his mother. His mother's dead. I'm only his aunt. He's my brother's child and my brother's in Saudi Arabia and I don't know what his blood group is.' Her voice rose hysterically again and it was obvious she was near to breaking point, but the clerk said soothingly, 'Well, as you're a blood relation just to know your grouping would be a help. Do you know it?'

'Yes, it's AB.'

'Thank you. And do you know if he's allergic to anything?'

Norrie sat down to answer and didn't feel Bruno move away so that they weren't touching. She answered the rest of the questions as best she could and the woman went away but came back later with two cups of tea before leaving them alone. Norrie didn't drink the tea, she just sat there holding it, her hand shaking so much that the tea spilled into the saucer until Bruno took it away from her, putting both cups on a small table in the middle of the room. Instead of coming back to sit down beside her, he crossed to the only window and looked out at the small garden surrounded on all sides by the tall buildings of the hospital wards. It wasn't until then, until Norrie looked at the square set of his shoulders, that she realised with a sickening kind of shock exactly what she'd done.

No need to think that he'd got to find out sometime;

to just dismiss him from Ben's life in the way she had must have been the cruellest way of all. He had been as desperately worried as she, and she had dealt him a killing blow. She had had to tell the truth, of course, there was no other way, but somehow she could have softened it, made it less hard. Only she was so worried about Ben that she hadn't thought of Bruno. Her eyes went to the double doors again, willing Ben to be all right, hoping that someone would soon come and tell her.

But it was nearly an hour before anyone came, the longest hour Norrie had ever gone through in her life. Bruno stayed but he didn't speak to her or sit close to her, picking up a magazine but obviously not reading it because he never turned the pages. Norrie wanted to say something to him, but there were other people in the room and this wasn't the time or place. And she wasn't even sure what she wanted to say even if she could have found the words. When the sister finally came into the waiting-room and walked towards them, Norrie stood up and felt Bruno do the same behind her, but again he didn't touch her. She was afraid to ask and couldn't speak, but Bruno said, 'How is he?'

The sister smiled, she actually smiled. 'He's doing very well. We've X-rayed him and he has no broken bones but he has concussion.'

'And his leg?' Norrie asked anxiously.

'He's had to have stitiches, but luckily he didn't lose too much blood and a transfusion wasn't necessary. We're going to keep him in tonight, but you'll probably be able to take him home tomorrow.'

Norrie felt such a wave of relief that she rocked on her feet and the nurse put out a quick hand to catch her. 'I want—I want to see him,' she managed to say.

'He's been given a mild sedative and is fast asleep,

but you can go and take a look at him. This way. He's in the children's ward.'

Ben was sleeping peacefully, still very pale but nowhere near as white as he had been. He had kicked off his covers as usual and they saw the white bandage covering almost the length of his leg. Slowly Norrie reached out and pulled up the covers, hiding the terrible wound from their sight if not from their minds. Very, very gently she brushed his hair from his forehead and bent to kiss him, blinking back tears of overwhelming relief. She straightened and looked at Bruno who was standing on the other side of the cot-bed. 'Bruno,' she began tentatively, 'I want to . . .'

'Don't say anything,' he interrupted her harshly. 'Not after what you've done to this child.'

Norrie stared at him with startled eyes. Was he blaming her for Ben's accident? But he had every right, she blamed herself entirely and would go on doing so for the rest of her life.

A nurse came up and began to draw the curtains around Ben's bed. 'I should leave him to rest now,' she advised, so they had to go, Norrie looking back reluctantly.

'Couldn't I stay here?' she asked. 'I'd like to be with him when he wakes. He'll want me.'

'We don't have the room, I'm afraid. And he will probably sleep through until the morning. 'Phone as early as you like and we'll tell you when to come.'

So there was nothing left to do but leave with Bruno. Outside the hospital he called a taxi and they sat in a taut, electric silence all the way back to the flat. But once there, Bruno erupted.

'You lying little slut! How *dare* you tell me that Ben was mine?' he yelled savagely.

'I didn't. I never said he was yours.' Norrie

hurriedly backed away from his fury into the sitting-room but he came striding menacingly after her.

'But you damn well let me think it.'

'No. I told you at the beginning that he was nothing to do with you.'

'Do you think that excuses it?' He caught hold of her arm above the elbow so tightly that she gave a cry of pain. 'You deliberately deceived me and you know it. You never attempted to tell me the truth. You never even once said that you weren't his mother. My God, I could kill you. You've used me and you've used that child just because you couldn't bear to think that you didn't have my total love and submission. *That's* what hurt you and that's why you've been trying to hurt me.'

'That isn't true, I . . .'

'Isn't it?' He took hold of her other arm and shook her. 'What do you really care about those people I sacked from the *Westland Gazette*. Have you ever been to see them or bothered to find out about them? Well, have you?' he shouted savagely.

Norrie stared into his furious face, appalled by his anger. 'No,' she admitted slowly.

'No. That's how much you care. But I have. When you told me just why you'd married me, I decided to find out for myself if I really had injured those people as much as you said. And do you know what I found? That five of them had got new jobs within weeks, one had taken the opportunity to emigrate to Australia to be near his family, and the other two had pooled their redundancy money to start a small business which is flourishing so well that they're more successful now than they ever were. And it's for them that you've uprooted Ben and made him unhappy.'

'I—I didn't know.'

'You mean you didn't damn well care.'

'All right.' She suddenly started shouting back at him. 'So maybe I did it for my father. You can't pretend that giving him the sack was a blessing in disguise. He's dead and . . .'

'Yes, he's dead, but Ben's his grandson and he's very much alive—luckily. Do you really think your father would have wanted you to do this to him?' His grip tightened and he pulled her up against him so that he was glaring grimly down into her face. 'But I don't think that you were even doing this for your father. You did it for yourself and no one else. You wanted to hurt me and I gave you the opportunity because I thought I was Ben's father. How you'd enjoy the kick in the teeth I'd get when you finally told me that he wasn't mine. Tell me,' he bit out savagely, 'when did you plan to do it? Did you have some nice little ploy set up to give me the maximum hurt, in front of a crowd of people presumably. Boy, I bet you were really disappointed back there at the hospital when you had to come out with the truth and the only person to see my humiliation was just one unimportant hospital clerk.'

'Let go of me.' His words had struck home, crashing through the barrier of hate she'd built up over the years, but the truth about her own actions was too devastating to take in all at once. Especially in the face of his anger. She needed to be alone, to have time to think.

She tried to pull free of his hold, but Bruno mistook her reasons and said furiously, 'Oh, no, you're not getting away that easily. You owe me. My God, how you owe me.' And he began to drag her towards the bedroom.

'No!' Her startled cry was lost as she struggled to get free. 'No, Bruno, please.'

He laughed harshly, a laugh that frightened her more than his shouting had done. 'It's too damn late to start appealing to my better nature. And Ben isn't here as a protection now. I've wanted you again for a long time and now I'm going to damn well take what I want.'

'No. Let me go.' Norrie began to fight him in earnest, angry that he couldn't see that it was all wrong, furious that he should try to force her. 'You animal,' she raged at him. 'Take your filthy hands off me.'

It was the wrong thing to say. If she'd reasoned with him he might have listened, but calling him an animal was like a red rag to a wild bull. Picking her up, Bruno carried her, struggling and yelling, into the bedroom, then started pulling off her clothes, tearing them in his impatient fury.

'You swine!' Norrie lashed out at him, her nails raking his face, not afraid any more but just plain angry.

They fought frenziedly, taking out their fear and relief over Ben on each other. Norrie swore at him, calling him everything she could think of, but Bruno was grimly silent, intent on winning. Her blouse tore open down the front, the buttons flying off, and then she staggered and lost her balance as he tugged her skirt down. She fell on to the bed and Bruno smiled grimly as her legs flew up and he was able to drag off her skirt and throw it aside. His smile infuriated Norrie even further and as he reached out to take off the rest of her clothes, she kicked out at him, catching him in the ribs.

'You wildcat.' He threw himself down on top of her but Norrie dodged sideways and they both landed up on the floor. Bruno pinned her down with his weight and, catching hold of her arms, held them over her head. His angry eyes glowered down into hers as she yelled at him, but then he lowered his head and took her mouth, cutting her off in the middle of an expletive.

She tried desperately to move her head away but he deliberately pressed down hard, hurting her lips, so that she couldn't move. So then she tried to bite him, but he forced her mouth open, violating it.

It was difficult to breathe with his weight fully on her and his mouth over hers, and it only made things worse when she struggled, so that at last she had to give in and just lie there. He didn't let up until she had lain without moving for some time, taking his fill of her mouth, using it as he wanted. Then he rolled off her, picked her up and dropped her on the bed. For a few minutes she lay gasping for breath and didn't start to react again until she saw that Bruno had taken off most of his clothes. Immediately she rolled towards the other side of the bed, but he grabbed her and hauled her back, pulling off her bra and pants. She fought him again then, but he was too strong and too angry. His dark eyes flamed with savage rage as he bore down on her, but there was lust there, too, now, and round his mouth a bleak determination.

Norrie cried out and struggled as he took her, but Bruno held her down as he thrust his body forward. 'You owe me,' he grated into her ear. 'You owe me this.'

She tried to bite him, to squirm away, anything. She could feel him and her whole mind wanted to scream in outrage. But then her traitorous body took over and somehow she wasn't moving against him any more, but with him. Tears gathered in her eyes and she began to cry. Her hands went to his shoulders and her body arched under him. 'It's been so long,' she mumbled brokenly. 'Oh, God, it's been so long.'

They made love as if there would be no tomorrow, as if that night was the last in the world. They didn't talk because words would have shattered their fragile truce. It was much, much too soon for words. Norrie lost count of the number of times they made love, but each was different. Bruno continued to use her roughly at first but as the hours went by he became more gentle, and once she opened her eyes and saw his face lit by the moonlight streaming through the uncurtained window. The anger was gone and in its place there was open need and longing. She wanted to speak to him then, to ask him to forgive her, but was afraid of only rearousing his rage and brutality and so stayed silent.

It wasn't until morning that Bruno slept. Norrie lay beside him looking at him for a long time, but then she slid out of bed, careful not to disturb him, showered and dressed. For a few minutes she hesitated, looking at his sleeping form outlined by only a thin sheet, but then she squared her shoulders and moved quietly around the flat, packing her own and Ben's things. At seven, she let herself out and took a taxi to the hospital.

Ben was awake, and the way anxiety vanished from his face to be replaced by a wide grin when he caught sight of her, was one of the most wonderful things that had ever happened to Norrie. He immediately started chattering away about the nurses and the hospital and the bandage on his leg, and seemed to have no memory about falling out of the tree, for which Norrie was thankful. She saw the sister and made arrangements for him to go to a hospital near Welford to have his stitches out and then carried him outside to the waiting taxi. 'We're going home,' she told him.

He looked at her questioningly. 'Home to Bruno?'

'No, back to our own home. To the cottage.' She sat back in her seat, holding Ben on her lap even though her body ached there and felt bruised, and he settled comfortably against her, content now to sit quietly, so she was able to close her eyes, and remember.

Biting on the end of her pen, Norrie sat at her desk frowning down at the printed forms in front of her. It was Ben's adoption papers and she'd run into a snag. They wanted to know the name of her next of kin. Ordinarily she would have written in her brother's name, but Geoff hadn't even seen Ben since he was a few weeks old and could have no feelings for him if he was so willing to give him up. But there was one other person who had loved him, even if it was for a short time. But would Bruno still love him now that he knew Ben wasn't his? It was a problem she had been pondering over for three days, but she really must send the papers back tonight. Suddenly making up her mind, Norrie wrote in Bruno's name and address, and filled in 'Husband' where it asked for the relationship.

Well, he was still her husband, for the time being at any rate. She had had no word either from him or his solicitors saying that he wished to file for an annulment—but no, it would have to be a divorce after that last, tempestuous night together. Norrie sighed and sat back in her chair, glad that it was done. She'd tried to get a job at three different places today and her feet ached. The car Bruno had bought for her had been left behind in London and all the jobs on offer seemed to be miles from a bus stop. After folding the forms and putting them in an envelope, she moved over to an armchair and kicked off her shoes. It was getting dark and she ought to close the curtains and put the light on, but she couldn't be bothered. Neither did she have the energy to turn on the television set, and it was too early to go to bed. She was going through the physical actions of taking up her old life, but it all somehow seemed pretty pointless at the moment. Everything did since she'd realised what an utter fool she had been. Her second chance with Bruno had been thrown away out of sheer stupidity and baseless hatred. If only she could go back to that first day when he'd walked into the *Welford Observer* just as she was going out. It could all have been so different. Norrie rather thought that she was going to go on thinking 'if only' for the rest of her life.

She thought about Bruno as she did most of the time, wondering what he was doing; if he was going out with that girl Katie, whether he'd had the wallpaper stripped off the room he had decorated specially for Ben. Tears of self-reproach and regret pricked her eyes and ran down her cheeks and she let them lie, too lethargic even to brush them away.

It was almost dark when a knock sounded sharply at the door, startling her out of her reverie. Glancing out of the window she stood stock still as she saw Bruno's Jaguar parked at the kerb. Her emotions were immediately so chaotic that she was strongly tempted to pretend that she wasn't in, but then hastily rushed into the kitchen to splash water on her face and rub it dry before going to the door.

He was wearing a dark suit and had a pale yellow rose in his buttonhole that reminded Norrie vividly of the bridal bouquet he'd bought her. Quickly she lifted her eyes to his face but his features were set into a harsh mask with only the deeper etched lines around his mouth betraying the emotional upheaval he'd gone through in the last few months.

'May I come in?' he asked stiffly when she didn't speak.

'Oh! Oh, yes.'

She stood aside and he walked ahead of her into the sitting-room, which was still in darkness. Nervously she switched on the light and he turned to face her. 'This won't take long.' His eyes flickered for a minute as he looked at her face, then were quickly veiled again. 'How is Ben?'

'He's fine. Thank you. He's had his stitches out and the local hospital are very pleased with the way his leg has healed.'

'Good, I'm glad. Perhaps you'd give him—my love.'

'Yes, of course. I'm afraid he's been in bed some time, but if you want to go up and see him . . .'

Bruno shook his head. 'No. I deliberately waited until he must have gone to sleep. I didn't want to disrupt him again.' He hesitated for a long moment while Norrie waited, guessing what was coming. But she had guessed wrong. 'And you?' Bruno asked harshly. 'Are you pregnant?'

Her startled eyes met his. 'What?'

'The last time I never checked to find out whether you were or not. I don't want to make the same mistake again,' he told her harshly.

'Oh, I see.' She looked away. 'No, I'm not.'

He let out a small sigh. 'I suppose I ought to thank you for telling the truth this time.' She didn't answer or look at him and he turned to go. 'That's all I came to find out.'

Opening the door he was about to step into the hall when Norrie burst out, 'I wish I was.'

He turned slowly back. 'Sorry?'

'I wish I was. Pregnant, I mean. I—I would have very much liked to have had your child.' She bit her lip, then said, 'Ever since Ben was given to me to take care of I've wished that he was yours and mine.'

Bruno was looking at her grimly. 'What are you trying to say?'

'That I'm sorry, I suppose. Both for now and for four years ago. I've been incredibly naïve and stupid, I know that, and I don't expect you to forgive me or—or anything, but I'd like you to know that I'm sorry.'

'Do you really expect me to accept that—or even believe it?' he asked harshly.

'No.' She turned away. 'No, of course not. I'm sorry, I shouldn't have said anything. I should have realised that you're not interested.'

He was silent for what seemed an age and then said, as if the words were torn out of him, 'I was interested for a long time.' Norrie hunched her shoulders waiting for him to tell her just what he thought of her now, then spun round to face him incredulously as he went on, 'And I find that some things just don't change, no matter what.'

'Are you saying that . . . Oh, Bruno, are you saying that . . .'

He gave a rueful, lop-sided kind of grin. 'I don't know what I'm saying. I only know how I feel. And that's incredibly lonely and empty. Even you doing your damnedest to make me miserable was better than coming back to an empty flat every day. It isn't home any more.' He broke off and looked at her wryly.

'Nor is this,' Norrie admitted. 'Even with Ben. He—he often asks about you. He misses you, too.'

'Too?'

She nodded and took a gulping breath. 'I was sitting here tonight in the dark, thinking about you.'

'You'd been crying.'

'Yes. At my own stupidity mainly,' she said on a broken, wretched laugh. 'I was so unhappy and so mixed up.'

'Don't let's have an inquest,' Bruno said sharply. 'It's over and the best we can do is forget it if we're to have any chance of trying again.'

For a moment her heart seemed to stop beating and then start again very rapidly. 'Can we—are we—going to try again?'

'It might be possible. But first we've got to get one thing straight; what about Ben? When is your brother coming back for him?'

'He isn't.' Going to her desk, Norrie found Geoff's letter and showed it to him.

'So you're going to legally adopt the boy?'

'Yes.'

'And where do I come in?' he asked grimly, still not sure that he wouldn't get a rebuff.

For answer she picked up the sealed envelope addressed to Geoff's solicitors, her heart thankfully glad now at the choice she'd made. 'Go ahead, open it,' she invited, handing it to him.

He gave her a quick, surprised look and then did as she asked. 'You put my name down?' he said incredulously.

'Yes, because you loved Ben and my brother never did. I knew that if anything happened to me you would take care of him and love him for himself, not because you had to.'

Carefully he folded the forms and put them back in the envelope, then laid it aside and turned towards her. 'Come here.'

Slowly she obeyed and shuddered as he put his arms around her. 'Oh, Bruno, I love you so much. That night . . .'

She couldn't go on, but there was no need. 'I know, it was for me, too; the most wonderful night of my life.' He smiled down at her. 'Bar one.'

Tears cascaded down her cheeks. 'Will you ever forgive me?'

'Forgive you? I think I just did. But I don't think I'll be able to forget for a long time, so just don't ever remind me, Norrie. Don't ever remind me.' He held her close, letting her feel his strength and love, and led her over to the settee and sat with her on his lap, gently kissing away her tears. But it was quite some time before he picked her up and carried Norrie up the stairs, to start their married life all over again.

Coming Next Month In Harlequin Presents!

839 BITTER ENCORE—Helen Bianchin
Nothing can erase the memory of their shared passion. But can an estranged couple reunite when his star status still leaves no room for her in his life—except in his bed?

840 FANTASY—Emma Darcy
On a secluded beach near Sydney, a model, disillusioned by her fiancé, finds love in the arms of a stranger. Or is it all a dream—this man, this fantasy?

841 RENT-A-BRIDE LTD—Emma Goldrick
Fearful of being forced to marry her aunt's stepson, an heiress confides in a fellow passenger on her flight from Denver—never thinking he'd pass himself off as her new husband!

842 WHO'S BEEN SLEEPING IN MY BED?—Charlotte Lamb
The good-looking playwright trying to win her affection at the family villa in France asks too many questions about her father's affairs. She's sure he's using her.

843 STOLEN SUMMER—Anne Mather
She's five years older, a friend of the family's. And he's engaged! How can she take seriously a young man's amorous advances? Then again, how can she not?

844 LIGHTNING STORM—Anne McAllister
A young widow returns to California and re-encounters the man who rejected her years before—a man after a good time with no commitments. Does lightning really strike twice?

845 IMPASSE—Margaret Pargeter
Unable to live as his mistress, a woman left the man she loves. Now he desires her more than ever—enough, at least, to ruin her engagement to another man!

846 FRANGIPANI—Anne Weale
Her sister's offer to find her a millionaire before they dock in Fiji is distressing. She isn't interested. But the captain of the ship finds that hard to believe....

H·A·R·L·E·Q·U·I·N

FIRST·CLASS
Sweepstakes

OFFICIAL RULES

1. NO PURCHASE NECESSARY. To enter, complete the official entry/order form. Be sure to indicate whether or not you wish to take advantage of our subscription offer.

2. Entry blanks have been preselected for the prizes offered. Your response will be checked to see if you are a winner. In the event that these preselected responses are not claimed, a random drawing will be held from all entries received to award not less than $150,000 in prizes. This is in addition to any free, surprise or mystery gifts which might be offered. Versions of this sweepstakes with different prizes will appear in Preview Service Mailings by Harlequin Books and their affiliates. Winners selected will receive the prize offered in their sweepstakes brochure.

3. This promotion is being conducted under the supervision of Marden-Kane, an independent judging organization. By entering the sweepstakes, each entrant accepts and agrees to be bound by these rules and the decisions of the judges, which shall be final and binding. Odds of winning in the random drawing are dependent upon the total number of entries received. Taxes, if any, are the sole responsibility of the prize winners. Prizes are nontransferable. All entries must be received by August 31, 1986.

4. The following prizes will be awarded:

   (1) Grand Prize: Rolls-Royce™ *or* $100,000 Cash!
   (Rolls-Royce being offered by permission of
   Rolls-Royce Motors Inc.)

   (1) Second Prize: A trip for two to Paris for 7 days/6 nights. Trip includes air transportation on the Concorde, hotel accommodations...PLUS...$5,000 spending money!

   (1) Third Prize: A luxurious Mink Coat!

5. This offer is open to residents of the U.S. and Canada, 18 years or older, except employees of Harlequin Books, its affiliates, subsidiaries, Marden-Kane and all other agencies and persons connected with conducting this sweepstakes. All Federal, State and local laws apply. Void in the province of Quebec and wherever prohibited or restricted by law. Winners will be notified by mail and may be required to execute an affidavit of eligibility and release, which must be returned within 14 days after notification. Canadian winners will be required to answer a skill-testing question. Winners consent to the use of their name, photograph and/or likeness for advertising and publicity purposes in conjunction with this and similar promotions without additional compensation. One prize per family or household.

6. For a list of our most current prize winners, send a stamped, self-addressed envelope to: WINNERS LIST, c/o Marden-Kane, P.O. Box 10404, Long Island City, New York 11101

Here's how to get this special offer from Harlequin!

As simple as 1…2…3!

NOVEMBER
TREASURY EDITION
COUPON

1. Each month, save one Treasury Edition coupon from your favorite Romance or Presents novel.
2. In four months you'll have saved four Treasury Edition coupons (<u>only one coupon per month allowed</u>).
3. Then all you have to do is fill out and return the order form provided, along with the four Treasury Edition coupons required and $1.00 for postage and handling.

Mail to: Harlequin Reader Service

In the U.S.A.	In Canada
2504 West Southern Ave.	P.O. Box 2800, Postal Station A
Tempe, AZ 85282	5170 Yonge Street
	Willowdale, Ont. M2N 6J3

RT1-D-2

Please send me my FREE copy of the Janet Dailey Treasury Edition. I have enclosed the four Treasury Edition coupons required and $1.00 for postage and handling along with this order form.

(Please Print)

NAME _____

ADDRESS _____

CITY _____

STATE/PROV. _____ ZIP/POSTAL CODE _____

SIGNATURE _____

This offer is limited to one order per household.

This special Janet Dailey offer expires January 1986.

SUPPLIES LIMITED

Take 4 books
& a surprise gift
FREE

SPECIAL LIMITED-TIME OFFER

Mail to   **Harlequin Reader Service®**

In the U.S.
2504 West Southern Ave.
Tempe, AZ 85282

In Canada
P.O. Box 2800, Station "A"
5170 Yonge Street
Willowdale, Ontario M2N 6J3

YES! Please send me 4 free Harlequin Presents® novels and my free surprise gift. Then send me 8 brand-new novels every month as they come off the presses. Bill me at the low price of $1.75 each ($1.95 in Canada)—a 11% saving off the retail price. There are no shipping, handling or other hidden costs. There is no minimum number of books I must purchase. I can always return a shipment and cancel at any time. Even if I never buy another book from Harlequin, the 4 free novels and the surprise gift are mine to keep forever.

Name   (PLEASE PRINT)

Address   Apt. No.

City   State/Prov.   Zip/Postal Code

This offer is limited to one order per household and not valid to present subscribers. Price is subject to change.   DOP–SUB–1